Blame it on Beauville?

This small Texas town has sure seen its share of romances! Elizabeth and Jake fell in love in *Blame It on Cowboys* (Temptation #802).

Then Jess fell in lust with Lorna in *Blame It on Babies* (Temptation #819).

What's going to happen now that Kate has come home to Beauville—and has to face her high school sweetheart? Rumors are flying fast and furious. And the whole town is watching for what unfolds next....

The tale continues in...

KRISTINE ROLOFSON

The author of nearly thirty bestselling books for
Harlequin, Kristine lives in Rhode Island. Married
and the mother of six, she began writing when
two of her children were only in diapers. She also
worked as a secretary, seamstress and waitress,
but her passions have always been writing and
travel. Known for her Western heroes, sense of
humor and strong female characters, this talented
author gathers readers wherever she goes.

Kristine enjoyed creating the fictional town of
Beauville and the host of characters who play out
their lives there. Look for her next outstanding
miniseries in Temptation beginning August 2001.
Montana Matchmakers is about a small town in
Big Sky Country that holds a matchmaking festival
each year. Enjoy!

Books by Kristine Rolofson

HARLEQUIN TEMPTATION
653—THE BRIDE RODE WEST
692—THE WRONG MAN IN WYOMING *Boots and Booties
712—THE RIGHT MAN IN MONTANA *Boots & Booties
765—BILLY AND THE KID
802—BLAME IT ON COWBOYS *Boots and Beauties
819—BLAME IT ON BABIES *Boots & Beauties

HARLEQUIN PROMO
MY VALENTINE
A TOUCH OF TEXAS
TYLER BRIDES

KRISTINE ROLOFSON

BLAME IT ON
TEXAS

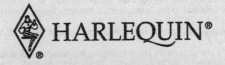

HARLEQUIN®

TORONTO • NEW YORK • LONDON
AMSTERDAM • PARIS • SYDNEY • HAMBURG
STOCKHOLM • ATHENS • TOKYO • MILAN • MADRID
PRAGUE • WARSAW • BUDAPEST • AUCKLAND

ISBN 0-373-83462-4

BLAME IT ON TEXAS

Copyright © 2001 by Kristine Rolofson.

All rights reserved. Except for use in any review, the reproduction or utilization of this work in whole or in part in any form by any electronic, mechanical or other means, now known or hereafter invented, including xerography, photocopying and recording, or in any information storage or retrieval system, is forbidden without the written permission of the publisher, Harlequin Enterprises Limited, 225 Duncan Mill Road, Don Mills, Ontario, Canada M3B 3K9.

All characters in this book have no existence outside the imagination of the author and have no relation whatsoever to anyone bearing the same name or names. They are not even distantly inspired by any individual known or unknown to the author, and all incidents are pure invention.

This edition published by arrangement with Harlequin Books S.A.

® and TM are trademarks of the publisher. Trademarks indicated with ® are registered in the United States Patent and Trademark Office, the Canadian Trade Marks Office and in other countries.

Visit us at www.eHarlequin.com

Printed in U.S.A.

CHAPTER ONE

"BIG NEWS," MARTHA announced into the phone. She cradled the receiver between her shoulder and her chin and hoped her daughter appreciated the effort. Kate never seemed to be overly interested in the goings-on in her hometown now that she lived in New York City, but Martha continued to keep her up with the news. Since the girl had spent more than a few hours at the drive-in with her friends when they were all growing up in Beauville, Martha knew Kate might find this worth listening to.

"Good news or bad news?" her daughter asked, sounding cautious.

"I've got the paper ready right here," Martha said. "I'll read it to you."

"Why don't you just tell me?"

Martha ignored the request. She was better at reading than telling and maybe this way Kate wouldn't ask questions her mother couldn't answer. "The former site of the Good Night Drive-

In will soon become a senior citizens' residence,'' Martha McIntosh read aloud.

"What? The drive-in's *gone?*"

"It sure is." And good riddance, too, Martha added silently. She'd watched the digging with more trepidation than most, but now that the concrete was poured she'd decided this was for the best. Her daughter's complete attention caught at last, Martha repeated the article's first sentence and added a few more details. The article was on the front page of the *Beauville Times,* but tucked down at the bottom, on the left, beneath the weather predictions and beside an article about the town council passing the school board's budget. "There's a nice drawing here, too. It's going to be real nice. They started construction this week and they're moving right along."

"That's so sad," Kate said.

"That old place was an eyesore, honey. And we could use something nice to look at, like the Good Night Villas. I thought Gran might move into town and into one of the apartments."

"Why?"

"Why?" Martha echoed, running out of patience. You'd think a twenty-seven-year-old woman would understand that an elderly woman shouldn't live twenty miles outside of town. "She's almost ninety, Kate. She needs taking care of."

"Does she want to move?"

"She's thinking about it," Martha hedged. If Gert Knepper had wanted to move off the Lazy K, she would have packed up her things and driven her truck to town. It didn't matter that she'd lost her driver's license twelve years ago or that she could have all the help she needed by picking up the telephone and asking for it, Gert did things on her own. When she decided to move, she'd appear on the doorstep with her suitcase.

"Right," Kate laughed. "I can't picture her anywhere but on the ranch."

"These apartments or condos or whatever they're called are going to be very nice. Carl said—"

"I guess I can't picture retirement 'villas' in Beauville."

Martha thought they sounded lovely, with everything new and clean and on one level. Carl Jackson was building them, on land he'd inherited from his father. Old Man Jackson had owned most everything in town once upon a time. He'd roll over in his freshly dug grave if he knew his son had become a land developer. "I'm thinking of buying one."

"Why?"

"Because I might be ready for a change." She could picture Kate frowning into her coffee cup. She'd heard the beep of the microwave a few seconds before. Kate was a caffeine addict, and these Sunday morning phone calls were usually punctuated by the sounds of Kate grinding beans, pouring coffee or reheating cups of the stuff. Always on the move, that one. Couldn't even sit still long enough to talk to her mother without reaching for some stimulation. Martha worried about her, wondered what she did for fun, wondered why she liked the city and her big important television job. Wondered if she'd find a nice man and have babies and bring them home to Texas on holidays so Martha could fuss and cuddle.

"That would be a pretty big change," she said. "What does Gran think of all of this? How is she feeling?"

"You'll see for yourself at the party. You're still coming, aren't you? They're not going to make you work on your vacation again?"

"No," Kate said, but there was some hesitation in her voice that made Martha nervous. She knew all too well how Kate's fancy New York City boss expected her to be on call. "Are you sure Gran's okay?"

"That old gal is as stubborn as ever," Martha said, wondering how on earth Gert could live out on the ranch much longer. Sometimes Martha had nightmares about her mother falling down the stairs or tripping over a cat. Gert looked tough, but at that age she had to be fragile. She should be pampered, should sell the ranch that no one in the family wanted to live on but Gert and use the money to take care of herself. "I tell her all the time she could live like a queen here in town if she'd just sell out."

"I'm not sure that's what she wants."

"The Foresters left and went back to New Mexico."

"She told me. She said she put an ad in the paper to get more help. Did she find someone?"

"She did, but I have my doubts."

"Why?"

"Do you remember the Jones family? You went to school with some of the boys, didn't you?" Martha didn't wait for an answer. Of course Kate remembered the Jones boys. Everyone knew that family and the trouble they'd gotten into. One of the boys was in prison. "They were a wild group of kids."

"What about them?"

"She hired one of them to help her out. He and his son moved in last week."

"Which one?"

"What?" Martha tore her gaze away from the front window. She could have sworn she saw Carl's white Cadillac pass by the house. She wondered if he would stop in and say hello, maybe take her for a drive the way he had last Sunday after church.

"Which one?" Kate sounded as if she was gritting her teeth.

"Not the oldest, but the other one. Dustin."

"Damn."

"What?"

"Nothing. Just a spill."

"Run cold water over it. Are you burned?"

"Not really. It mostly went on my robe." She laughed softly. "You'd think I'd learn not to do ten things at once."

"You and your grandmother are so much alike, always busy," Martha said. She watched as Carl put his Cadillac in reverse and guided it into a parking spot in front of her house. "I'd better get going," she added. "I've lots to do today."

"But Mother," her daughter said, "we haven't talked about Gran's birthday party."

"Later," Martha told her. "I'll call you later." With that, she hung up. He'd promised to take her to see the latest developments on the condos. He'd also promised frozen margaritas and more than a little flirtation.

Martha loved being retired.

"YOU COULD HAVE warned me," Kate said, sipping a cup of freshly brewed coffee. She pushed aside the *New York Times,* all eighty pounds of it, in order to have more room on the table. "Mom started talking about the Good Night Drive-In and all I could think of was what we were doing there with our boyfriends when we should have been watching the movies."

Emily's Texas drawl was still as strong as ever, even through the phone. "I meant to," she said. "I was gonna mail you the newspaper, but I was afraid you'd think you were growing old and get all depressed and lose your fancy job and become one of those New York City bag ladies."

"Very funny. Don't you think it's depressing?"

"Honey, depressing is being pregnant for the fourth time in nine years. Sex at the drive-in with Dusty Jones was a hundred years ago."

Kate didn't want to think about sex. Or having babies. Or Dustin Jones, the one boy her parents had forbidden her to date. The one her grandmother had hired to take care of the Lazy K. "My grandmother just hired him."

"Hired who? I mean, whom?"

"Dustin."

"No kidding?"

"He and his son are living out on the ranch."

"I didn't know he got married."

"He got Lisa Gallagher pregnant that summer before college." The summer from heaven, Kate remembered. The summer she'd made love to Dustin Jones in the back seat of his '72 Buick. "I don't think they ever got married."

"No, they didn't, but I'll ask George. He'll

know. I wonder what happened to Lisa. I always thought she moved to Dallas.''

''It doesn't matter,'' Kate lied. Of course it mattered. After all these years she damn well wanted to know what happened after she left town.

''I thought he was working for Bobby Calhoun out at the Dead Horse Ranch. But I never heard he had a boy with him.''

''My mother seemed pretty sure. I can call my grandmother and find out if it's true. If she answers the phone.'' Gert generally disliked having to stop what she was doing to talk to ''some darn salesman.''

''I'll see you in two weeks, right? You're coming home to help blow out the candles?''

''I wouldn't miss it,'' Kate declared, though she wondered if she could stay the entire two weeks as she had originally promised. There was a whole team of scriptwriters for the show, but that didn't make her workload any lighter.

''What's going to happen next on *Loves of Our Lives?* Is Harley pregnant with Dan's baby or Christian's?''

Kate laughed. ''You know I can't tell you.''

''I'm afraid I'll have the baby and miss finding out.''

''When are you due?''

''In two weeks. Right now. Yesterday.''

''And?''

"Not an ache or a pain anywhere, Kate. Plan to spend some time over here, will you? You and George can gripe about progress and teenaged memories. He doesn't like the idea of his drive-in destroyed for a nursing home either. He says it makes him feel like an old man." Emily and George had dated since they were fifteen, married at twenty and become parents at twenty-two.

"At least someone understands."

"Honey, the minute we all ran out and bought VCRs, the days of the drive-in were numbered. The Good Night lasted longer than most, I think, just because Mr. Jackson never cared if it made money or not."

"I suppose. But it's still sad." She took another sip of coffee before continuing. "My mother said she's thinking of moving into one of the apartments."

"Give him the truck, Jennie, and quit teasing," Emily scolded, then apologized. "Sorry, Kate. They're little devils this morning."

"Where's George?"

"At the grocery store. He figures this is all Carl's fault."

"What is?"

"The Good Night Villas. Every single woman— over sixty, that is—figures the way to Carl's very single heart is to buy one of those apartments.

George's mother wants to put her house up for sale.''

"I think mine does, too." Now she had to worry about her mother being taken advantage of by a real estate Romeo? "Do you think we'll be like that in thirty years?"

"Alone and running after Carl Jackson? I hope not."

"At least thirty years from now you won't be pregnant," Kate teased. "That's something."

"Come home soon, honey. We'll sit in front of the air conditioner and talk about boys, just like we used to."

I could do that, Kate wanted to say. *I could pretend I was eighteen and in love and letting a certain young cowhand unbutton my blouse while* Last of the Mohicans *played on the distant screen.*

"What's New York have that Texas doesn't?" It was the way Emily ended every phone call, and Kate usually replied by telling her friend about her latest date or Manhattan meal or Broadway show. Emily loved all of the advantages of city life, but this time Kate didn't answer the question.

"I wonder if my mother is serious about moving," Kate muttered. "She even wants my grandmother to move in there with her."

"You'll be here soon. You can find out for yourself. Hey, you can even see how Dustin Jones turned out."

I might not have a choice, Kate wanted to say. Even though I'd rather be run over by a speeding taxi and dragged down Broadway with my skirt up over my head.

"IF THAT'S MARTHA again, tell her I'm not home." Gert carried her bowl of oatmeal over to the kitchen table and sat down to eat it. The boy hurried over to the east wall and grabbed the phone off the hook.

"Hello?" A smile turned up his mouth. "Oh, hi."

"Who is it?" she asked.

"It's my dad."

Well, that was all right, Gert figured, giving Danny a nod before she turned back to her oatmeal. She should have put chocolate chips in it, the way she did for the boy. She didn't bother trying to listen to the conversation and instead looked through the stack of last week's mail for something to read. The *Beauville Times* sat there taking up room, so Gert checked through it for the obituaries before she read the headlines.

The Jackson boy was still determined to build those fancy apartments, she noted. Cattle prices had gone up, but not much. The weather was going to be good. Good and hot, she saw, but heat was the least of her worries. The heat didn't bother her much, not like that darn air-conditioning folks

stuck everywhere. Give her a good fan. Now there
was a healthy invention for you.

"I remember that summer in '22," she said
aloud. "Now there was a heat wave," she told
Danny, who had hung up the phone and approached the table. "It was so hot my daddy swore
we'd all just dry up and blow to Oklahoma."

The boy slid into the chair across from hers and
smiled. He sure had a sweet smile, Gert thought.
Not like his daddy at all that way, but then boys
didn't always take after their fathers. Sometimes
they got lucky and forged their own paths.

"Did I ever tell you I had a boy like you once?"

He nodded. "Yes, ma'am."

"Always in trouble, Hank was." Gert figured
he'd gotten it from his father's side of the family,
of course. Back in the twenties, the Johnson boys
had been hell on wheels. Her father had just about
had apoplexy when she'd run off with one of them.

"Where does he live now?"

"Oh, he's been gone a long time. He could
never stay in one place for too long." She tilted
her head at him. "I'll bet you've never even been
to a drive-in movie, have you?"

He shook his head. "I don't think so."

"You don't even know what it is. That's too
bad." Gert worked on her oatmeal for a moment,
then peeled a banana, broke it in half and offered
a section to Danny. Another morning ritual, they

shared a piece of fruit before the day really got started, before chores. Sometimes she fixed coffee mixed with heavy cream and lots of sugar for the two of them. Sometimes the boy's father would come in and pretend to complain that his eight-year-old son was too young to be drinking coffee.

"I saw some women on television the other day," Gert continued, knowing Danny liked the sound of her voice. He was a funny little guy, this boy. "They'd written a book about the 'old days,' Katie Couric said. Now they're rich and on the bestseller list and everyone's buying their book."

"Cool."

"I could use the extra money," Gert mused. "Why don't you get us some orange juice?" The boy did as he was told, as he usually did. He got stubborn about taking a shower and sometimes she could hear him yelling about it. That yelp always made Gert smile to herself and remember Hank when he was little and still lovable. And still all hers.

"Thank you very much," she said, when he delivered the glasses of juice. It was important to teach the young people manners. Seemed like not too many folks thought of that these days, but folks should learn them just the same.

"I've got some money," Danny said. "Twenty-one dollars."

"Ooh-wee, that's a lot of money," Gert told him. "How'd you get all that?"

"I worked for my dad. A lot."

"Good for you. That's how folks are supposed to get money. By earning it, just the way you did." She watched him beam with pride. He was going to be a handsome boy, probably on the small side, though his father was tall and lean. They both shared dark straight hair and brown eyes. Handsome devils, the two of them, with identical dimples in the center of their chins. That Dustin could have his pick of the women in the county, she was sure, but he didn't mind her teasing him about it.

Gert liked teasing. Her Edwin never minded a good joke, laughed even harder when the joke was on him. That was a good quality in a man.

"I should write a book," she said, taking a sip of the juice when the boy did. "Those other old ladies did real well with theirs. Maybe there's a market for memoirs."

"Memoirs," the child repeated, trying out the unfamiliar word.

"Memoirs. That's like memories," she said. "The story of somebody's life. I've had a pretty interesting life, I think." Or maybe not. Maybe nothing special to anyone else, but she was partial to it.

"I could spice it up a bit," she thought aloud. "Add some old lady wisdom, too. Folks like that, at least in books." But not in person. Martha didn't take too kindly to advice lately, despite her carrying on with the Jackson fella and talking about "villas" and "central vacuuming," whatever that was. Meant you didn't have to sweep anymore, Gert supposed.

"Sweeping's good exercise," she told the boy, who didn't seem to mind the change in subject.

"You want me to get the broom?"

"No, thank you. Not on Sunday. We're not doing chores on Sunday."

"Oh." He looked down at his juice glass, then back at her. "Dad's doing chores."

"Well, that's because your daddy's a hard worker and likes to get things done."

"Yep."

"What'd he want on the phone?"

"Just to check to see if we were okay."

"Well," Gert said, looking around her old kitchen with its worn linoleum and scarred cabinets, "I think we're doing just fine, don't you?"

Danny's dark eyebrows rose. "That's what daddy says all the time." He lowered his voice and repeated, imitating his young, serious father. "I think we're doin' just fine."

Gert couldn't help chuckling. "Well, we are. I don't know why everybody worries so much."

The boy shrugged. "Me neither. You want some more juice?"

"No, thanks. But you help yourself. And there's more biscuits in the bread box over there."

"Okay."

Gert watched him, just for the pleasure of it. It was sure nice to have a youngster around to talk to. To have anyone to talk to, though Danny's father wasn't much for chitchat. She squinted at the clock over the refrigerator. Kate would call today, and she'd be coming home soon for the party.

Maybe she would start writing that book this week so she could surprise her granddaughter with Chapter One.

CHAPTER TWO

"MY DAUGHTER WANTS me to move in to one of those things with her," Gert declared as they drove past the sign announcing the site of the Good Night Villas.

"I guess no one can force you," Dustin said, slowing down the truck so Mrs. Knepper could get a good look. She'd insisted on coming here first, to see for herself the latest change in the town. "Can they?"

"I sure hope not."

"You want me to stop?"

"I sure do."

"Cool," Danny said, tucked in the narrow length of seat behind them. "I like this."

"I'm glad you're having a good time." Dustin wasn't at all sure why he was driving around Beauville on a Monday morning when there was all sorts of work to be done on the ranch, but she was the boss and so here he was on the north edge of town looking at a drive-in where he'd spent a lot of nights panting after Kate McIntosh. Maybe the fascination with drive-ins ran in the family.

He pulled into a dirt area alongside the road, but kept the motor running for the air-conditioning. He didn't want this nice little old lady passing out from heatstroke. "There. How's this?"

"Just fine." She rolled down the window and stuck her head out as if she was going to yell at the construction workers. Not that anyone would've heard, with a dozer moving dirt around behind the foundation. A blast of dusty hot air wafted into the truck, but the elderly woman seemed oblivious to it as she watched the construction crew of five men erecting framework. "They don't move too fast, do they."

"It's the hottest part of the day," he pointed out, hoping she'd close that window before she expired from the heat and the dust. It scared him, how old she was. "Maybe you should—"

"They can take their time, for all I care. I'm in no hurry to die in one of those silly villas." She sighed. "I'll bet you spent a few nights in this place. Or are you too young to remember the drive-in movies on weekend nights?"

"I remember." Darkness. Kissing Kate. Pressing her down on the back seat, the one with the rips in the vinyl he'd taken great pains to repair. To this day duct tape made him think of making love to a brown-haired teenaged girl.

"My family used to keep cattle here, back before the railroad came through. Did you know that?"

"No, ma'am."

She pressed the button on the door and the window rolled up. "My, that's easy."

"Yes." He waited a moment. "Are you ready to head back to town, Mrs. Knepper?"

"I think you'd better call me Gert. We should be on a first-name basis since we live together."

"And me?" the boy said, leaning forward so that his chin touched Gert's shoulder for a brief moment. "What can *I* call you, Mrs. Knepper?"

"Mrs. Knepper," his father replied.

"Well, now, most of the children I know call me Grandma Gert, so you sure can, too, Danny," Gert declared. "If that's okay with your daddy."

Dustin nodded and put the truck in reverse. "Where to now, Gert?"

"The library, I think. I have some books to get and then we'll get groceries after we go to the bank."

"Sure."

"Danny can go to the library with me and help me carry the books," Gert said. "You must have errands of your own to do without dragging an old lady around with you."

"I'm worried about the heat, Gert. You want to get a cold drink at the café first?"

"I wouldn't mind. The boy and I might have one of those chocolate milk shakes."

Danny got a kick out of that idea. "Oh, boy," he said, leaning forward again. "I never had one of those before."

"Well, my goodness." Gert was clearly speechless. She frowned at Dustin. "Does he have one of them milk allergies or something?"

"Not that I know of." He didn't know much, that was certain.

"What's that?" the boy asked.

"It means you get sick when you drink milk or eat ice cream, things like that," Dustin explained, hoping he was right. No one had warned him that becoming a father meant you were supposed to be right about everything.

"I'm okay," Danny insisted. "Grandma Gert and me've been drinking milk all week."

"We sure have," the old woman agreed. "So I guess a chocolate milk shake will go down real good—with some French fries and maybe a hamburger, too."

"Wow," the child whispered under his breath. Dustin winced, wondering what in hell Lisa had done to this kid besides the crap he already knew about. Too thin and too quiet, Danny still had that scared look in his eyes, like someone was going to yell at him or worse. Dustin felt sick to his stomach and his hands clenched the steering wheel.

Gert gave him a sharp look. "You'd rather be back at the ranch working, wouldn't you?"

"Well, ma'am, there's a lot that needs doing." Not that any of it would matter if Gert decided she'd lived out there for too long. He could always go back to the Dead Horse and work for Bobby Calhoun, but what would he do with the boy? Growing up in a bunkhouse was no place for a kid, and it was long past time to get started on making some kind of home for the child. And for himself.

"I thought maybe I should be running more cattle."

"You've got the grass," he agreed.

"Well, see to it, Dustin. Maybe we'll try to make some money this year."

He nodded. "Yes, ma'am. We sure could, though it might take me more than a year. I've come up with a plan for the cattle and the grass but it's not short-term."

"A plan is good," Gert agreed. "Making some changes is good, too. You grew up around here, didn't you?"

"Yes, ma'am. Outside of Marysville."

"But you know my granddaughter, Kate."

"Yes." Intimately.

Unfortunately.

KATE WAS LATE. And there would be hell to pay, along with the possibility of missing seeing her grandmother blow out the candles on her birthday cake. Kate could do without the crowds and the fruit punch and the photographer from the *Beauville Times,* but she hated to disappoint her mother and grandmother, especially when they looked forward to her visits so much. And she looked forward to the peace and quiet of her hometown.

She hurried through the airport toward the car rental booths. Already hot and uncomfortable, she was ready for the arctic temperatures of her rental car. She'd brought her suitcase to the office, just in case, but there hadn't been time to change into something less businesslike than a black suit and shell-pink camisole. It had been another hellish week on *Loves of Our Lives,* which made getting home even more difficult.

Everyone in town would be at the party. The grange hall would be filled. She wondered for the hundredth time if Dustin would be present or back at the ranch taking care of things there. Odd that Dustin Jones would end up on the Lazy K, along with his son, who must be eight now. Seeing Dustin wouldn't bother her, she decided, signing the papers to rent the biggest, fastest Lincoln available. She would be polite, of course. She scooped up the keys and the directions to the Alamo lot and hurried toward the wide doors that fronted the sidewalk. She would pretend that nothing had ever happened between them, that he hadn't broken her heart and made her feel like the biggest fool in Texas.

"THERE SHE IS," Gert declared, pointing to the door. "You can rest easy now, Martha. Our girl is home."

"Thank goodness." She hadn't realized she'd been so tense and worried, but she worried when she knew Kate was flying. She always listened to the hourly news reports on the radio just to make sure there hadn't been a plane crash, even though she knew Kate would call her when she was safe in her apartment or hotel room. There was always that span of time when she didn't know if Kate was safe, that span of time when she prayed a lot. Maybe that was the trouble with having only one child. You couldn't spread the worry around. "I wonder what happened."

Gert shrugged. "Doesn't matter, Martha, as long as the child gets here safe and sound."

"She's not a child," she said, watching her beautiful daughter make her way toward them. Her hair was streaked gold and fell in fashionably tousled lengths to her shoulders, her elegant black pantsuit made her look like a movie star, or like those women in the magazines with perfect lipstick and jewelry and fingernails. "She's too thin."

"You always say that."

"It's always true. She works too hard."

"We'll fatten her up," Gert promised. "I made cinnamon rolls this morning."

Martha frowned at her mother. "In this heat?"

"I got up early. Couldn't sleep."

"Too much excitement," Martha declared, leaning down to make sure her mother didn't look too tired. No, Gert looked pleased, a woman who had reached the age of ninety and lived to tell about it. The blue-flowered dress with the pearl necklace looked good on her and the pink lipstick had been a nice touch. Too bad her mother wouldn't agree to getting her hair done yesterday.

"Go rescue her," the older woman said. "Joey will talk her ear off."

"He always liked her. I don't know why she didn't give him a chance. Now he built that nice house south of here and—"

"The feeling wasn't mutual," Gert said, giving Martha a little push. "I'd do it myself but it'll take me too long to get out of this chair. This crowd's got me blocked in."

"All right," Martha said, needing little encouragement to greet her child. "Joey doesn't look as if he's making much progress."

"Ha," Gert sniffed. "It'll take a stronger man than—oh, hi, Esther. Thank you for coming."

Martha left her mother talking to one of her longtime friends from church and, careful not to get any punch spilled on her as she walked through the crowd of Beauville residents, went to her daughter.

"Mom!" Kate waved and said something to Joey, probably promising to stop by his store this week. As if Kate wouldn't prefer to buy her fancy jewelry in New York.

"Kate, I'm so glad you're finally here. I was so worried," she said, giving her daughter a quick hug. "You've lost more weight."

"You always say that," she said, sounding exactly like her grandmother.

"Well, it's true."

"I'm sorry I'm late. We had a problem with the show and I had to fix it before I could leave, and then my flight out of Kennedy was delayed two hours because of rain and—"

"They work you too hard," Martha said, leading her toward Gert, who was presently surrounded by well-wishers and unable to be seen through the crowd. "You need this vacation."

"I can't wait," she said. "I'm so glad to be home and—"

"Martha? You look terrific, as always." She turned to see Carl beaming at her. Not a tall man like her Ian, Carl was at eye-level. It was somehow comforting, not to have to look up to see into a man's eyes.

"Thank you," she said, trying not to sound flustered. "You know my daughter, don't you?"

He shook Kate's hand. "Of course. Kate. Your mother tells me all about your TV show and your life in the big city."

"Oh?" Her eyebrows rose, but Kate was as polite as she always was. Not many people could tell what Kate was thinking behind those calm hazel eyes. "I've heard about your plans for the drive-in, too."

"Not plans anymore, Kate. *Reality*. We've poured the foundation." Carl moved closer to Martha, which thrilled her more than a little, though she didn't want Kate to get the wrong idea.

"If you'll excuse me," Kate said, "I need to wish my grandmother a happy birthday."

"You just arrived?" Carl asked, standing so close to Martha that their arms touched.

"Yes." Kate gave her mother a questioning look. "Are you coming, Mother?"

"Of course. We'll see you later, Carl," she said, patting his arm just a little bit before she followed her daughter to see Gert.

"Welcome home," he called after them.

Kate paused. "Mother, is that man—"

"Here, honey," Martha interrupted, not about to discuss her personal life in a hall filled with everyone in town. And Kate used "Mother" when she had something serious to discuss, another reason to hurry her along. She nudged her daughter

through the crowd of senior citizens that surrounded Gert.

"Grandma," Kate said, smiling down at her
grandmother, whose face lit up with matching happiness.

"Well, well, come give me a hug," Gert said,
struggling to rise out of her chair. Several people
hurried to help her, so for a moment there was
some confusion until Kate was in her grandmother's arms and embracing her. Martha blinked
back tears. It was so good to have her daughter
home again. If anyone could talk sense into Gert,
it would be Kate. After all, she was the smartest
person in the family, the most successful and the
one with all the answers. If Kate said, "It's time
to move to town," then that's what Gert would do.
She and Martha could have side-by-side suites at
the Good Night complex.

"Did I miss the birthday cake?" Kate asked.

"You think I'd blow out ninety candles without
my favorite granddaughter here to help me?" She
motioned to Martha. "What do you think? Can we
do it now?"

"I'll get it started, but it's going to take a few
minutes to light."

Kate moved toward her. "I'll help."

"No." Martha shooed her away. "See if you
can find Jake. I saw him a little while ago, but his
wife looks like she's going to have that baby any

time now, so I imagine she's sitting down.'' Martha scanned the room, then pointed to the west corner of the building. ''I see him.'' She tried to catch his attention, but her nephew, deep in conversation with a group of men, didn't see her wave. Well, Kate would take care of it. The cousins—half-cousins, actually—always seemed glad to see each other, and Gert's other grandchild needed to be in on the birthday cake presentation.

Martha hurried toward the kitchen, picking up volunteers along the way, along with compliments about Kate's appearance. Her girl had done well. And gotten what she'd wanted. Martha missed her, but that was the way life was. Children grew up and moved away, and mothers made their own lives.

Their *new* lives.

CHAPTER THREE

SHE WAS HOME. Turning cartwheels in the middle of the grange wasn't an option, though tempting. Her black pantsuit, with its fashionable amount of spandex fabric, could withstand the exercise but she didn't know if her mother's heart would tolerate the shock. As a child, she'd been notorious for turning cartwheels any time that joy overtook her and she could no longer keep all the happiness inside. As an adult, she had to be content with smiling. She was home, in Beauville, where everything was safe and familiar. Including her handsome cousin who turned, waved and headed over to meet her in the middle of the room.

"What are you smiling about?" Jake put his arm around her shoulders and hugged her against his side. "Are you that glad to be back home?"

"Of course. And I'm happy to see you," she said, planting a kiss on his cheek. "I hear you're going to be a father very, very soon."

"Any day now." He beamed and glanced back

at his wife, who saw Kate and waved. Elizabeth
seemed to glow, though she looked about to burst.

"It's too hot in here, Jake. Take her home."

"Soon," he said. "Neither one of us wanted to
miss seeing a cake with ninety candles on it. I
guess we're doing it now?"

"I came to get you, for the pictures."

"Sure, but I have to get Beth. I don't dare let
her out of shouting range these days."

Kate followed him, wishing she knew Elizabeth
better. They'd married last summer, but Kate
hadn't met her until Christmas, and even then there
hadn't been much time to really get to know each
other. All Kate knew about her cousin's wife was
that she was from Rhode Island, she had no family
of her own except a grown niece, and had offered
Kate the use of her east coast beach house anytime
she wanted to use it.

"You know Dusty Jones, don't you?" Jake
asked, as a lean dark-haired man stood on the other
side of Elizabeth and helped Jake get her to her
feet.

"Yes," Kate said, intending to glance at him
only briefly. He was taller than she remembered,
though the wide shoulders and lean build were the
same. She avoided meeting his gaze, sensing he
wasn't any more pleased to see her than she was
to see him. She would have thought that nine years
would have made them both immune to bad mem-

ories, but maybe there were some things that just stuck, no matter how much time had passed.

"Hello, Kate," Dustin said, but he looked at the pregnant woman beside him. "There, Elizabeth. I guess we got you on your feet okay."

"I knew I shouldn't have sat down," the woman chuckled. She reached for Kate's hand. "Kate. It's so good to see you again."

"And I'm glad to see you," Kate said, "but are you sure you should be in the middle of all of this right now?" Elizabeth looked as if she was expecting triplets, and she looked flushed. Kate made a mental note to turn up the air-conditioning.

"Don't worry." Elizabeth smiled and patted her enormous belly. She wore a mint green sundress and, despite her rosy cheeks and damp bangs, looked like a model for elegance during pregnancy. "I've promised Jake I'd let him know when the first twinge begins. I didn't want to have to leave before Gert saw her cake, though, but so far so good. Oh, I almost forgot," she added. "Emily wasn't feeling well this morning and thought she'd better skip the party. She asked me to tell you she would call you tomorrow."

"Do you think she's going to have the baby today?"

Elizabeth shook her head. "I don't know, but if she beats me to the delivery room I'm going to be very, very jealous."

"I didn't know you two knew each other so well," Kate said, realizing that the two women had more in common with each other than they did with her. She fought another twinge of envy for Elizabeth's pregnant glow.

"Yes. And I want you to meet Emily's neighbor, Lorna Sheridan." Elizabeth tapped a petite blond woman on the shoulder. When she turned, Kate saw that the woman held a baby in her arms. Both had light yellow curls and blue eyes, and both were beautiful. The baby wore a cute blue-and-white striped sunsuit, so Kate assumed he was a boy. "Lorna, I'd like you to meet Jake's cousin, Kate McIntosh."

Lorna smiled and adjusted the baby in her arms so she could shake Kate's outstretched hand. "I've heard so much about you. I used to live across the street from Emily and she talked about you all the time."

"Oh," Kate said, realizing that this was the woman who had married the sheriff last winter. "Emily went to your wedding," Kate remembered.

"Yes. She and Elizabeth helped me out a lot."

"And your husband's the sheriff."

"Who's working today," she added. "He hated to miss the party, but he couldn't help it."

"You have a beautiful baby. How old is he?"

"Four months." Lorna smiled again. "He just started sleeping through the night."

"I hope mine is as good as this little one here," Elizabeth said, touching the baby's soft head with her fingertip. "Lorna's let me baby-sit so I could practice being a mom."

Kate had the unsettling fear that all of this baby-making might be contagious. Beauville appeared to be a hotbed of fertility. She was rescued from panic when Jake tapped her on the shoulder.

"They're lighting the candles now," he said, "so we'd better move over to the dessert table."

"Daddy?"

Kate glanced past Elizabeth to see a young dark-haired boy tugging on Dustin's calloused hand. His son. Of course. He was a miniature version of his father, though small for his age.

"What is it, Dan?" Dustin's tone was patient, as if he was used to answering the boy.

"Grandma Gert said I could help."

"With what?"

"The candles," he said, sounding almost timid. Kate would have expected any Jones child to be hell on wheels. The entire family had had a wild streak the size of the Rio Grande. "She said I could help blow them out if she didn't have enough air."

Jake reached over and tousled the boy's hair. "Well, you'd better come on. She's my grandma, too, and Kate's. So we'd better get over there pronto.''

Dustin hesitated, frowning a little. It didn't diminish those looks, Kate saw, watching from a few feet away. Elizabeth, standing next to her, held out her hand to the child. ''Danny, can you take my hand? I could use some help.''

Danny looked up at his father.

''Go ahead,'' Dustin said. ''But walk slow. Mrs. Johnson has to take it easy.''

''I know,'' he said, sounding more like his father with that Jones confidence. Kate moved out of the way so the boy could accompany Elizabeth, flanked carefully by her husband. Kate joined the group just as Dustin moved to follow his son and Kate found herself in the awkward position of walking with him toward the front of the room.

She couldn't think of a thing to say. A woman who had most likely written hundreds of thousands of words of dialogue in the past four years couldn't come up with her own script. What do you say to an old lover? Kate couldn't imagine, could only hear her own words of nine years ago, *get out*. Funny, she wished she could say that again, so he would turn around and leave the building and that would solve everything. And what did that say about her own emotional maturity if her reaction to this man was still the same? Not much, she decided. Kate attempted to paste a smile on her face as various townspeople greeted her and said they were glad she was here for "the big day," but she was conscious of Dustin walking so close to her.

Pathetic, she told herself. It's been nine years and being close to him still makes my heart race. Her mother would have a fit when she saw him, which was the only vaguely humorous thing in this whole encounter.

Unfortunately, Martha was too busy rearranging the dessert table to notice the man she had once described as "the wild, no-good Jones boy" who would date her daughter "over my dead and lifeless body." Then her attention was taken by Elizabeth and Jake, and Gert's delight over their presence at the party was clear to see. Kate watched the small boy shyly approach her grandmother, but Gert put one arm around the boy's thin shoulders and hugged him close to her.

"You remembered, did you?"

He smiled a little, as if afraid to be too happy. "Yep. I've never seen so many candles before."

"Neither have I," her grandmother said. "Do you think I can blow them all out?"

"I'll bet you can," Kate replied, stepping closer. She would not let Dustin's presence here ruin such a special occasion. "If you have enough help."

Gert smiled. "Kate, have you met my buddy Danny?"

"I sure have. He looks ready to help, and—"

she caught her mother's frantic wave by the
kitchen door right before someone turned off the
lights "—here it comes now."

Someone began to sing "Happy Birthday" and
everyone joined in as the three-layer cake was
wheeled across the room and placed in front of
Gert, who looked as if she was enjoying the celebration. Kate blinked back tears and tried to sing
as she watched her grandmother's expression of
delight. Dustin's deep baritone rang out, reminding
her that he'd liked to sing along to the radio as
they drove around the county, looking at ranches
and land and talking about their dreams.

Well, she'd dreamed of loving someone who
wouldn't get someone else pregnant. When that
didn't work out she'd dreamed of getting out of
town. Getting out of Texas.

"Now?" Danny asked, as soon as the singing
stopped and the crowd waited expectantly.

"Now," Gert declared, and Kate edged closer
to help if she was needed. Jake, on the other side
of Gert, gave Kate the thumbs-up signal. "One,
two, *three!*"

It took a few tries, but the four of them managed
to get the candles extinguished.

"Did you make a wish, Gert?" someone called
out from the crowd. Carl Jackson, Kate noticed,
because he winked at her mother after he asked the
question.

"Sure did," Gert replied, dipping her index finger into the butter cream frosting and taking a taste. "But don't ask me what I wished for, because I'm not allowed to tell, am I, Danny?"

"Nope."

"Take a lick."

The boy dared a glance at his father, who must have nodded his permission, because Kate watched him dip a tentative finger into one side of the cake and take the tip off of a pink rose and stick it in his mouth. Yes, Kate thought, watching him. Charming the women, just like his father. Daring to take what he wanted and damn the consequences.

"*Kate,*" her mother hissed, as if she had grown impatient saying her name. "Pay attention. I need you to help cut the cake."

"Sure," she said, picking up one of the knives readied for the task. "Any special directions?"

Her mother frowned. "Yes. Cut the pieces small and keep your mind off that cowboy."

"I'll try to cut the pieces small," Kate promised. "And I don't have any idea what cowboy you're talking about." Dustin had moved to the other side of the table where he could supervise his son. She watched as he bent down and said something to Gert that made her chuckle.

"Ha," Martha said, placing a stack of small

rose-decorated paper plates in front of her. "You and Gert. Cut from the same cloth."

"I know."

"You'd better pay attention to what you're doing or you'll cut your fingers off with that knife," her mother said.

"Don't worry," Kate said, slicing the top layer of the cake into neat squares. "I know what I'm doing."

"Yes," her mother sighed, scooping cake slices onto plates with a sterling server. "You always thought you did."

Kate bit her tongue to keep from saying something she would regret. Her mother could turn a self-assured television writer into a cranky teenager with only a few sentences. Kate smiled to herself. Maybe that's how she'd inherited her flair for dramatic dialogue.

"Give that piece to your grandmother," her mother said, pointing to the section of cake with the most frosting. "She still has a sweet tooth."

"All right."

"And make sure Elizabeth gets some cake and doesn't have to wait. I imagine Jake wants to get her home and off her feet."

"Okay." She looked for Jake and, when she caught his eye, pointed to the cake. He nodded and came around the back of the table.

"You need help with that?" He started to take the knife from her hand.

"No, Mom wanted to make sure that Elizabeth had cake before you left."

"You should take her home soon," Martha advised. "She should be resting."

"That's what I told her too, Aunt Martha, but she's got a mind of her own."

"She's lovely," her mother said, nodding approvingly toward the pregnant woman sitting on a metal chair near Gert. She handed Jake a piece of cake. "Here, make sure she eats something. And don't forget there's lemonade and iced tea, too, in case she's thirsty."

Her cousin winked at Kate and took the plate that was almost as big as the piece of cake it held. "Yes, ma'am. I'll take good care of her."

"Such a nice couple," Martha murmured. "I don't know why you can't find a nice man like that in New York."

"Neither do I," Kate said, which was her standard reply every time her mother stated this particular complaint.

"You work too hard."

"Yes."

"Well, now you're on vacation. You can get some rest."

"And keep my mind off cowboys?" She couldn't help teasing.

"Good Lord, I hope so."

Kate had to laugh, but she watched Jake deliver cake to his wife, noticed Lorna cradling her baby while an elderly woman talked to her, saw Dustin take his son in hand so other well-wishers could talk to Gert, and she felt another stab of envy. She was home, so why all of a sudden did she feel like a stranger in her own town?

HE'D BE DAMNED IF he was going to stare at Kate McIntosh, but then again, she sure looked good. Too thin and too pale, as if living in the city wasn't healthy. Tense, too. The way she gripped that cake knife meant trouble for anyone who got in her way. Her mother was probably aggravating the hell out of her. Some things didn't change.

He heard his son giggle. And some things did. Like the fact that he was a father now, responsible for a child. He had to get the boy away from Gert before he ate so much frosting he'd be sick. No one could say this kid had the Joneses' iron stomach.

"Come on, Danny." He bent down to Gert, who sure looked as if she was enjoying her party. "You look pleased with yourself. Are you sure you don't have a bottle of Jack Daniel's in that old purse of yours?"

The old lady laughed. "Don't go broadcasting my secrets, Dustin. I'm just feeling real good, that's all. I survived almost a whole century. No one else in town can say that, can they? Poor Mike Monterro would have celebrated his ninetieth this month, too, if he'd lived that long.'' She sighed. ''So I guess I'd better be grateful about living so long.'' She gave Danny a kiss and thanked him for helping with the candles, then looked at Dustin. ''What do you think of my granddaughter?''

''She's very beautiful.'' No lie, even dressed in black and looking like a ghost, Kate was as gorgeous as she ever was.

''Yep. She's home for two weeks, you know.''

''Yeah. I know.'' Gert had informed him at least twice a day for the past month. He'd had time to figure out that ignoring Kate would be the easiest way to deal with her.

''She'll be coming out to the ranch.'' The old lady studied him as if waiting for a reaction. So Dustin didn't say anything, just waited for Gert to continue. ''You can show her what you've been doing.''

''I'm not real sure she'd—''

''Be interested?'' Gert finished for him, a mischievous glint in those pale blue eyes of hers. ''I think she would be.''

Dustin shrugged. Gert could think whatever she wanted, but it was time to drag Danny away from the cake. ''Come on, son. We've got chores to do.''

"It's Saturday afternoon," Gert protested. "You've got the rest of the day off."

"And, unless you need me to take you home, I'm going to spend a couple of hours putting a two-year-old quarter horse through his paces."

"Can I stay?" Danny looked up at him. "Please?"

"I'll watch him," Gert promised. "And Kate and Martha will bring us back to the ranch later."

"Sorry, buddy," Dustin told his son. "But I need your help this afternoon." He wasn't about to leave the boy with people he barely knew, not that he doubted Gert's good intentions.

"Excuse me." Martha McIntosh appeared behind Gert's chair. "The photographer is here for the pictures, Mother. He said you might make the front page."

"How about that." Gert grinned at Danny, who giggled. "I'm gonna be a star." She waved at the photographer, a thin young man who wore a serious expression. "Over here, young man. Do I know you? What's your name?"

He shook his head. "I just moved here, ma'am."

"Well, that's all right," she told him and tugged Danny back into her embrace. "Take a picture of me and my friend here."

"Is he your great-grandson, ma'am?" He focused, then counted to three. "Smile."

They did, and then Dustin tried once again to get Danny away from Gert and out of the grange hall.

"Come on, Danny. Let's let the folks get the real picture," he said, over Gert's objections. He eased the boy away as he saw Jake and Kate heading toward them.

"What about the cake? Grandma Gert said I could have a big piece. A corner piece."

"You haven't had enough frosting?"

Kate, holding two plates, handed one to Danny. "Here you go," she said, producing a white plastic fork to go with it.

He looked down at the cake, cut from the coveted corner, and then up at the dark-haired woman who had handed it to him. "How'd you know?"

"It was just a lucky guess."

"What do you say, Dan?" Dustin urged, wanting his son to make a good impression, and hating himself for wanting to impress this woman.

"Thank you. A *lot*."

"You're welcome." The smile she gave his son surprised him with its warmth. The visiting princess, dispensing favors to the little people. He wished the glamour girl would head back east, as far away from him and the boy as possible.

CHAPTER FOUR

"I MISSED SEEING Emily this afternoon. I need to call her tonight and see if she's okay." Kate dumped a stack of dirty paper plates into the plastic garbage bag and continued to clear the banquet tables. The ninetieth birthday party was over, the guests long gone, and three ladies from Gert's church were cleaning up the kitchen. All Kate had left to do was take out the garbage and help her mother wipe down the tabletops.

"When's that baby due?" Martha looked up from wrapping the leftover cake in plastic.

"Anytime now."

"Same as Elizabeth. It sure was a hot afternoon to be nine months' pregnant."

"Yes, it was. Jake's wife looked as if she needed a cool shower and a nap," Kate said, remembering how easily Dustin had helped Elizabeth from her chair. She wondered if he'd helped Lisa when she was pregnant. And if he'd married her. "Jake wanted to stay and help clean up, but I told him to go home and see that Elizabeth had some rest," she added.

"We'll have them out to dinner one night this week, unless she has the baby." Martha finished packing the leftovers into a cardboard box. "There. All done. Now all we have to do is find your grandmother."

"Last time I looked she was in the kitchen drying dishes."

"I told her to do nothing but sit down and rest."

Kate hid a smile and wiped off the last table. "She doesn't take orders very well."

"Neither one of you does."

"It runs in the family."

"Well, you didn't get it from me. You and Gert are an awful lot alike."

"Is that such a bad thing?" Her mother started to lift the cardboard box, but Kate stopped her. "I'll take that."

"Be careful," she warned. "Hold it from the bottom."

"I'll put it in the car while you get Gran. And I'll drive right up to the front door, so wait for me." Gert loved big luxurious cars, said they made her feel like a movie star.

"Oh, my," she said, ten minutes later as she settled herself on the front seat of the rented silver Lincoln. "I feel like Elizabeth Taylor. All I need is one of those big diamond rings."

"Oh, Mother," Martha said, chuckling from the back seat. "If you liked a big car so much, why didn't you ever buy one?"

"Your father never would buy anything but a Chevrolet, Martha. You know how he was." She peered out the window. "Are these tinted?"

"Yes," Kate replied.

"Power windows?"

"Absolutely."

"Just like Dustin's truck," Gert murmured. "I like riding in that, too."

"He's supposed to be working on the ranch," Martha pointed out. "Not out joyriding."

"I asked him to take me to town, Martha. I had some errands and—"

"I would have taken you," her daughter insisted. "I ask you all the time, 'Do you want to go to town, Mother?' don't I?"

"How is your car, Mom?" Kate attempted to divert the conversation. "Did you get those new tires you were—"

"I had private business," Gert insisted, ignoring her granddaughter's sigh. "Important business. In the library. And I wanted to see those villa places you're always yapping about."

"You went to see them?" Martha sounded almost delirious with relief. "Aren't they going to be lovely?"

Gert turned around and frowned. "It's a hole in

the ground right now, Martha. With cement. There wasn't anything 'lovely' about it at all.''

"I showed you the picture.''

Gert waved to Kate. "Drive us out there, honey. We'll take another gander at the place and see what it looks like. Your mother's real anxious to get us a couple of rooms there.''

"Well, maybe we should do that another day,'' Kate hedged. "You must be tired from the party. How about if we go to the Steak Barn for dinner? Do they still have those small filet mignons with the mushrooms and the baked—''

"I'd rather eat at home,'' her grandmother replied.

At the same time Martha said, "That would be nice, dear.''

Kate wondered which decision would get her into the least trouble. She wanted to laugh, but didn't dare. The familiar squabbling meant she was home again.

"It's your birthday, so you decide,'' Kate said, glancing toward her grandmother as she drove down Main Street. "We'll go past the drive-in and then turn around and take you home. How about if we pick up a pizza for dinner and take it back to the ranch? We'll go to the Steak Barn another night.''

"They do have an early bird special on Tuesdays,'' her mother said.

"Good. Pizza it is," Kate said.

"Better make that two pizzas," Gert said. "The boys and I can have the leftovers for lunch tomorrow."

"The boys?" Kate echoed.

"Dustin and Danny."

"Oh." So Gran fed the hired help now.

"He said he knew you when you were in high school."

"Yes. A little." She ignored the snort from the back seat. "How long has Carl Jackson been working on the retirement home project, Mother?"

"Not retirement homes, Kate," her mother corrected. "Senior villas. 'Independent living' is the phrase that Carl prefers to use."

"I'm living independently right now," Gert said.

"Mom, I can't believe you'd want to sell the house and move into a small place like that," Kate said. She'd pictured getting married in that house. Imagined her children visiting their grandmother in the enormous yellow kitchen.

"Honey, can you turn the air-conditioning down? I'm one big goose bump."

"Mother never feels the heat," Martha said.

Kate obediently turned the fan to "low," though the cold air blasting from the vents had been heavenly. She'd removed her jacket three hours ago and, even in a pink tank, had still been uncomfortably warm. "I guess it's going to take me a while to get used to the temperature again."

"It's not like this in New York?"

"Sometimes," she said, stepping on the gas as they left the main part of town and headed north. "Maybe not this hot."

"We have a nice breeze in the evening out on the ranch."

She eyed the air-conditioning dial and wished she could turn it to "high." "Your birthday party was wonderful, Gran." She raised her voice. "Mom, you did such a good job putting the party together."

"It was fun, wasn't it?" she murmured, sounding pleased with the compliment. "I have the guest book, so we can look at all the names later. And there were so many cards!"

"I think I'll put them in a scrapbook," Gert said. "That way I can keep 'em nice."

"Is this it?" Kate slowed down as they approached what used to be the drive-in. On the left side of the road was a large construction site and an enormous foundation.

"Yes," her mother said, leaning forward to point to the cement structure. "Isn't that going to be something?"

"It's going to be something," Kate remarked. "I'm not sure what, though." Kate turned into the makeshift parking area, but didn't turn off the engine. Surely they wouldn't want to sit here for more than a minute or two.

So much for the drive-in. The only recognizable fixture was the distant screen, its metal posts shining in the late afternoon sun. Her memories of this place were of sunset, waiting for the sky to darken enough so the movies could be shown. And then a broad black sky would surround them and the picture on the screen would practically pulse with color and then she and that young man she'd thought she was in love with would tumble into the back seat and pretend to eat popcorn until...

"—old enough to know my own mind," Gert was saying, having turned around to face her daughter in the back seat. "Besides, I've got plans of my own," she said.

"What kind of plans?" Martha asked. "I hope you mean you've decided to sell the ranch after all."

"Sell the ranch?" Kate echoed. "Why would you want to do that?"

"My plans are my own business," Gert said. "You'll both know them soon enough, but I think it's time I did something new. Something kind of exciting."

"My ninety-year-old mother wants excitement." Martha leaned against the back seat and closed her eyes. "Oh, Lord," she muttered. "Give me strength."

And give me a frozen margarita, Kate thought, turning the car around to head to the Lazy K. Add a pair of cotton shorts, a T-shirt and a view of the southwest grazing land and she'd be content.

"It's good to have you home," Gert declared, reaching over to pat her granddaughter's arm. "New York is too darn far away."

"Yes," Kate agreed, heading toward town. "Much too far." She hadn't been home for six months and in that time, both of the women in her family seemed bent on making changes. Her grandmother wanted excitement and her mother wanted the local real estate developer. Everyone else was having babies—she'd seen no less than seven pregnant women at the birthday party—and the drive-in was going to house retired seniors who'd be too busy making quilts and playing cards to remember watching movies at the Good Night Drive-In.

"WE NEED BEER." Gert shut the refrigerator and looked at her beautiful granddaughter. Kate had changed into a set of clothes she kept on the ranch, in the little bedroom that was always hers, and Gert thought she looked lovelier in those faded denim shorts than she'd looked in that black suit. She didn't like Kate wearing black. It reminded her of too many funerals. "Don't wear black when I die."

"What?" Kate opened one of the pizza boxes and plucked a piece of pepperoni off the top and plopped it in her mouth.

"No black. It's too depressing."

Kate laughed. "I'm going to be depressed when you die, Gran."

"Wear something pretty," Gert said. "None of those city gal clothes."

"Fine. No black suits." She saw Kate glance at Martha, who was too busy reading the paper to listen to what was going on. Martha would no doubt have an opinion, and three women with opinions in the same kitchen was downright dangerous. "Who wants pizza?" She reached into the cupboard and brought out three plates.

"I do, but I want a beer, too."

"Do you *have* any beer?"

"No. But I'll bet my foreman does. Go over to the bunkhouse and see if he'll loan me some."

Martha looked up from the paper. "Mother, since when did you start drinking beer?"

"I don't tell you everything," Gert said. "Just because I'm ninety doesn't mean I can't have secrets."

"Secrets, Gran?" Kate grinned at her. "Are you going to share?"

"Not yet. Go see Dustin, will you? And ask him and the boy back for pizza, too. There's plenty here to go 'round."

Kate hesitated, clearly displeased with the idea, which made Gert struggle to keep from chuckling.

"I'll go out and buy some," Kate offered, reaching for her purse.

"Nonsense. By the time you get back the pizza will be cold," Gert insisted, enjoying herself. Oh, she remembered a few years back when Martha was worried about an eighteen-year-old Kate. When the girl was sneaking out to meet some young cowboy and upsetting her parents. Her poor father, Ian, had had his hands full that last summer.

"We don't need beer," Martha said, putting the paper down. "I'll have a piece of that pepperoni pizza, Kate. Mother, why don't you sit down and get off your feet? I'll fix us a nice pitcher of lemonade."

"Never mind," Kate said, replacing her purse on the counter. "I'll see if I can find Dustin."

"Good. I've had enough lemonade for one day."

Kate kissed her grandmother on the cheek as she headed past her toward the door. "You should have what you want on your birthday."

"Well, for starters, you can settle down and make me a great-grandmother," she replied, giving Martha a wink. "That's what I'd like for my birthday."

"When I find a man, you'll be the first to know," Kate promised. Gert watched her granddaughter leave the kitchen, the screen door banging shut behind her.

"She says there's no one special in New York," Martha said, coming over to take Gert's arm. "Sit down, Mother. You're going to give me fits."

"There are good men here in town." Western men. Texas men. Men who knew about the land. "She sneaked out with Dustin Jones that summer, didn't she?"

Martha hesitated. "I never knew for sure. Then Ian died and Kate went off to college. There were rumors."

"And you thought it was him she was seeing?" How very, very interesting...and convenient.

"For a while, until he got some waitress in Marysville pregnant."

"Hmm," was all Gert could say to that, but she frowned.

"I didn't approve of Kate getting involved with a Jones," Martha said, settling Gert in the chair. "And I'm not sure I'd approve now, so don't go matchmaking."

"We could keep her here," Gert pointed out. "Right here in Beauville." Now she had her daughter's attention. "If we play our cards right. Maybe she'd like to move back home one of these days, take over your house in town when you move to the fancy villa place."

"Kate's life is in New York. She makes good

money, she has a good job and she likes her life just the way it is.'' Martha folded up the paper and set it aside. ''Let me get you a piece of pizza. You didn't eat anything but cake this afternoon.''

''That'd be good, Martha. Thanks.''

''And you're not fooling anyone with that beer nonsense,'' her daughter said, walking past her to the counter. ''I know you don't drink that stuff.''

''I'm going to start,'' she declared. Kate would do as she asked, hunt down that handsome young man and seek a favor for her poor old thirsty granny. He might smile down at her and Kate would be all businesslike, with that cool expression of hers.

These young people could be so foolish.

''BEER?'' DUSTIN LED the horse closer to the fence where Kate stood. She looked better now, he noticed, in clothes that didn't look as if she was trying to impress anyone. Her face was flushed, as if she'd been running. Maybe that's how she kept so slim in the city. He told himself he didn't care how she looked, wouldn't bother looking at her if she was stark naked and begging for his attention. ''Have you worked up a thirst this afternoon?''

''Beer,'' she repeated, looking exasperated. ''My grandmother seems to have a craving and asked me to ask you if you had any she could borrow.''

He laughed, and the horse raised his head and took a few steps backward. "Whoa there," he told him, but he looked over Kate's shoulder to make sure Danny was there. The boy never seemed to tire of pushing metal trucks around a hole he'd dug near the old water trough, and sure enough, he was still hunched over a yellow bulldozer. "I have a few bottles in the fridge. Do you know where I— we live?"

"No." And he could tell she didn't want to.

"Danny and I are in the largest bunkhouse."

"Not the foreman's house?"

"Too far away." Her eyes were still that odd shade of blue, with dark fringed lashes and eyebrows tilted like bird wings. "Gert needs someone to live close to the house."

"I see."

Dustin pointed to the bunkhouse, the one with the blue curtains in the windows that faced a front porch. "You can help yourself to the beer. I'm not quite done here."

"Thanks." She started to turn away, then stopped and looked over her shoulder. "Oh, I almost forgot. Gram wanted to know if you and...your son would like to join us for pizza. And beer." She smiled, just a little.

"Not tonight," he said. "But tell her thanks anyway."

"I will." She strode away from him, toward

the bunkhouse, and Dustin watched her step onto the front porch and open the door. Dustin wanted nothing more than to remind her that they'd made love. More than once. He wasn't a stranger she could walk away from as if they'd never spoken more than a few words.

He should have known he'd run into her. Obviously. Dustin fiddled with the horse's halter and pretended not to watch Kate leave the bunkhouse, two bottles of beer in her hand, and those long legs hurrying down the porch steps. He watched her round the corner of the bunkhouse and head toward her grandmother's.

"What did the lady want?" Dustin looked over the fence into his son's dark eyes.

"To borrow something."

"What?"

"Something to drink for Grandma Gert."

The boy smiled up at him. "She's pretty."

"Yes." The horse bumped him with its head. "I'll finish up here and then we'll go find us something to eat, okay?"

"Okay." Danny climbed on the fence and hung his thin arms over the top rail. "I forgot about supper."

"Me, too."

"What about Grandma Gert?"

He backed up the horse a few feet and began to let out the rope. "What about her?"

"Is she having supper?"

"Yep. With her family."

"*We're* her family, too," the boy insisted. "She told me."

"There's a lot of different kinds of family," Dustin said, but couldn't think of anything else to add to that. So he led the horse into the middle of the corral and urged him into a trot as he let out the rope.

Yeah, lots of different kinds of family, all right. The kind that beat the crap out of you for nothing and the other kind, the birthday party kind. *We're making our own kind of family* was what he should have told the boy, but truth was he wasn't sure he believed that himself.

CHAPTER FIVE

ONLY FOR HER grandmother would Kate have confronted the cowboy and asked for a favor. Tomorrow she would buy plenty of beer, replace Dustin's, and make sure her unpredictable grandmother would have all the drinks she wanted. For the rest of her time home, she should certainly be able to avoid the man, or at least act as if the sight of him didn't affect her.

And why should it? She was a different person, a woman with a life far from Beauville, Texas, and cheating cowboys.

"I don't know why you hired that particular young man," Martha said, when Kate returned to the kitchen with the bottles of beer.

"Why did you, Gran?" Kate flipped the cap from the bottle and tossed it into the garbage can by the ancient refrigerator. "I thought you were looking for another married couple."

"Or thinking again about a move into town," Martha said. "Which makes a heck of a lot more sense than living way out—"

"I'll move when I'm good and ready, Martha," Gert interrupted. "And it's not that easy to find help. Dustin's only been here a few weeks, but we're getting along just fine." She turned to Kate. "Honey, I don't need a glass. I'll drink it right from the bottle. It's more fun that way."

"You should have a cleaning woman, someone to help you here in the house all the time," Kate said, looking around the cluttered kitchen. She would clean while she was here, give the place a good scrubbing, wash the checked curtains, clean the windows. "I'm sure Dustin does his job outside, but you shouldn't be alone in here all day."

"The boy visits."

Martha rolled her eyes. "A little boy isn't the same as a housekeeper, Mother. You know that. And those Jones boys aren't trustworthy. Isn't the older brother in jail?"

"Jail?" Kate almost dropped her pizza in her lap. Gert ignored both questions and continued on as if it wasn't important or newsworthy.

"Dustin worked for Jake at the Dead Horse before he came here and Jake had nothing but good things to say about him."

"Why did he leave?" She plopped a piece of pizza on her grandmother's plate, then lifted a piece toward her mother.

"Thank you, dear," Martha said, reaching for her glass of iced tea. "That sure smells good."

Gert pulled her plate closer. "Mmm, thanks. He needed a place for the boy, he said. With Jake running his own spread and Bobby Calhoun on his own, the Dead Horse has gotten kinda wild."

"Bobby was always a character. He's still on the ranch, then?"

"Oh, my goodness, yes," Gert agreed. "Martha, do you remember when he was a little guy?"

"I sure do. Wildest kid in first grade."

Kate figured she'd earned a little prying. "What about Dustin's wife? Where is she?"

"I have no idea," Gram said. "I don't ask him much about his personal life, but he tries real hard with that boy of his. I don't think they've lived together very long."

"Why?"

She shrugged. "He's not real comfortable being a father, I guess. Sometimes the man looks like he doesn't know what to do or say to the boy. And little Danny seems in awe of his father, like he's on his best behavior all the time."

"Maybe he just got custody of the boy," Martha said, finishing the slice of pizza with one last bite. "I wonder who his mother is."

Kate knew. Lisa Gallagher. Lisa had been everything Kate had not been, including free to spend as much time as she wanted with Dustin and the rest of the wild Jones family. A year older than Kate, she'd been a waitress at a bar outside of town that summer. Which was why she'd calculated that Danny would be at least eight.

"Dustin's son is very small for his age," she said, not realizing she'd spoken aloud until her grandmother answered.

"He's a little thin, I guess."

He looks more like seven, she thought, thinking of the child actors she'd seen on the set of *Loves of Our Lives.*

"He's a nice boy," Gert declared, but Kate didn't know if she meant Dustin or his son, and decided not to ask. She'd had enough of Dustin Jones for one lifetime.

"Have you opened all your cards?" she asked, hoping to change the subject of the conversation. Her mother reached down and lifted a large wicker basket filled with pastel envelopes.

"Looks like you have your work cut out for you, Mother," she said.

"My, my, this will be fun," Gert said, taking another sip of beer. "Reading all of those might take me a week or two."

"And there are presents to open," Kate said. "They're in the trunk of the car. I'll bring them in as soon as we're done eating."

"My, what a day." Gert beamed at her granddaughter. "Having you home is the best present of all."

Kate blinked back sudden tears and leaned over to hug her grandmother. "I'm glad to be here."

"And we're glad to have you back," her mother added. "There isn't anything we've looked forward to more than that."

"Me, too," Kate managed to answer. "I'm always glad to be home." She left the older women and went out to the Lincoln under the guise of getting the birthday gifts. She really needed to breathe the thick, heated air and look up at the sky for a few moments of peace. New York seemed very far away.

"I WANT TO GIVE IT to her *now,*" the boy insisted, "cuz today's her birthday."

"It can wait 'til tomorrow," Dustin said. "She's got company."

"So?"

"So..." Dustin repeated, wondering how to explain without hurting the boy's feelings. Gert was with her family now. "It's not polite to interrupt when Gert has company, that's why."

"She won't mind," Danny said, pulling his sneakers on over his clean feet. He'd just gotten out of the tub and, instead of putting pajamas on, he'd dressed in clean clothes and figured he was going visiting. "Maybe they're gone and she's all alone."

No such luck, Dustin knew. He was able to see

the driveway of the main house from his second-story bedroom window. Kate's Lincoln was still parked there. How long was she going to stay in town? Long enough to talk Gert into a retirement home? Long enough to sell the ranch and kick him and the boy out? He'd tried this afternoon to ask Jake if he knew anything about his grandmother's future plans, but they'd been interrupted before he could get to it. Still, Gert had told him to buy more breeding stock, had given the green light to his ideas for improving the range lands, had agreed to tearing down some of the buildings that would blow down in the next storm. Gert had even hinted that she'd be willing to sell some shares of the Lazy K to the right man.

"Dad," the boy said, tugging on his sleeve as if to remind him that he was standing there. "She's gonna like it, right?"

"Sure she is, but—"

"Good." Danny, dressed in clean clothes that were too small for him, picked up the tissue-wrapped gift and gave his father one of his rare smiles. "This is the best part, you know."

"Best part of what?" They wouldn't stay long, wouldn't even move from inside the back door. They could be in and out in five minutes and then Danny would go to bed happy.

"Birthdays."

"And the best part is what, the presents?"

"Yep," the boy said, pushing the screen door open. "Can I have a party when I'm nine?"

"Sure."

Danny turned back toward his father. "Really? You mean it?"

"I'll do my best," Dustin promised, though he didn't know where the boy would be come fall. And he wasn't even sure when his birthday was, exactly. He'd have to find out without Danny catching on that he didn't know when the boy was born. Damn Lisa for this whole mess, he thought for the hundredth time. She'd no right to mess up the boy the way she had and leave other people to pick up the pieces, but that was Lisa. A more selfish, self-centered woman hadn't been born.

"Are you coming with me?"

Dustin hesitated. "You want me to?"

"Yes," the boy answered, his eyes big. "It's getting dark."

"Well, then I'm coming with you," he said, following the boy out the door and into the dusk. It was his favorite time of day, when chores were done and the wind had died down and everything seemed to be settled into place for the night. Kate and Martha should have gone by now, leaving Gert to go to bed. The old woman's lights were off before nine most nights and here it was almost that time now.

"I'm not really scared," Danny whispered,

waiting for Dustin on the porch. "You know that, right?"

"Yeah." He hid a smile. "I know that. Sometimes a guy just likes a little company at night."

"Yeah," the boy echoed. "Sometimes a guy does." They walked together in silence. "You think she'll like it, right?"

"Right."

"It smells."

"It's supposed to."

"Oh, yeah, I forgot." He sniffed the package. "Flowers, huh?"

"Roses."

"Okay. Roses, roses," he whispered to himself, trying to memorize the name of the scent, Dustin supposed. He escorted the boy to the back door of the sprawling ranch house and knocked against the peeling frame of the door. The whole place needed work. From sanding and painting the house and outbuildings, to repairing the cracked windows on the second story, to putting a new roof on the barn, the Lazy K needed a lot of work to lose its neglected appearance. If it were his...

It wasn't the first time Dustin had caught himself thinking that way, knowing that the amount of money he'd managed to save over the past few years while working at the Dead Horse wouldn't be enough for a down payment on the outbuildings, never mind the house and land. Still, if Gert was willing to sell shares, then maybe anything was possible.

"Come on in," he heard Gert call, and Danny was three steps ahead of him into the kitchen, the present clutched in his small hand and the birthday card scrunched into his jeans pocket, no doubt.

"Pizza," Danny declared, sniffing the air before hurrying over to where Gert sat at the table. "Happy Birthday," he said, and handed her the gift.

"My, my," the old woman murmured, reaching out to envelop the child against her. "This is too pretty to open."

"I wrapped it myself," he told her, with a shy look at Dustin. "My daddy helped a little."

"Not much," Dustin confessed, staying by the door. Kate wasn't there, but her mother was eyeing him as if he'd come to steal the silver. "I'm not very good at wrapping."

"Come sit down," Gert said. "Pull out a chair. Are you hungry?"

"No, ma'am, we ate already."

Martha rose and began to clear the table of the dirty dishes. "We have plenty of pizza left. And there's lots of cake, too." She surprised him by smiling at the boy. "I'll bet I could interest you in a piece of cake." Danny looked toward him for permission.

"Sure, go ahead," Dustin said, relaxing now that there was no sign of Kate.

"Coffee?" Martha McIntosh asked. "I was just going to make a pot. Decaf, though," she added.

"Thank you, but don't go to any—"

Gert waved her hand at him. "No one's going to any trouble, Dustin. My daughter's afraid I drank too much beer, so she's bound and determined to pour coffee in me." She winked at Dustin. "Isn't that right, Martha?"

"My mom drank too much beer," Danny said. "The policeman said—"

"Danny," Dustin interrupted, giving the boy a look he hoped would stop him from saying anything further.

"Well, she did," the boy said, lifting his chin as if daring Dustin to argue with the truth. "*Lots* of times."

"Let's see what's in this pretty package," Gert said, diverting the child from any more revelations. "How did you know I like pink?" He shrugged. Gert lifted the package to her nose. "Ooh-wee, this smells good."

"Roses," the boy announced.

"Roses? Well, how nice. I'd better open it up." She untied the bow and the tissue paper fell apart to reveal three bars of pink soap. Until Danny had spotted those in a Marysville gift shop, Dustin had had no idea that soap could be so expensive. Still, it wasn't much of a gift, not after what Gert had done for them. But Danny had insisted—the rose soaps or nothing.

"Do you like it?" Danny leaned over and helped move the tissue away so Gert could see the soaps, individually tied with pink satin ribbons.

"My, my, how beautiful. And these are too pretty to use," she declared. "But I think I will anyway, first thing tomorrow morning when I take my shower." She gave him a big hug and kissed his cheek. "Thank you so much, Danny."

"You're welcome."

"And you, too, Dustin," Gert said. "Thank you."

He opened his mouth to tell her it was nothing, but the kitchen door opened and he had to move out of the way or get hit with a load of shopping bags.

"Here," he said, reaching to take them out of Kate's arms. He should have known she would still be around somewhere. He couldn't be that lucky. "Let me take those."

"I've got them," she insisted, refusing to relax her grip on the bags she held in front of her like a shield. "If I let go of one I might let go of all three of them."

He backed off, but he didn't like doing it.

"Sit down, Dustin," Gert said. "You don't need

to hover by the door like that. We've plenty of room around the table.''

"Here, Daddy," the boy said, pointing to two empty chairs beside each other around the old oval table. "You sit here and I'll sit here."

He'd look like a fool if he refused, but he watched Kate navigate toward her grandmother and set the bags at her feet.

"There." She smiled down at Danny. "I'll bet you came over to have more cake."

"And to give me a present," Gert said, holding one of the soaps up. "Smell. Isn't that nice?"

"Mmm," she said. "Rose?"

"Yep," his smitten son declared, staring up at Kate with an eager-to-please expression. Dustin pulled out a chair at the table, when he really wanted to grab the boy and run for the bunkhouse. *Careful, boy,* he wanted to say. *She's the kind of woman who'll smile at you one day and break your heart the next.* "Oh," he said, reaching into his pocket to pull out a crumpled envelope. "I forgot this."

"Oh, my," Gert said, taking the envelope. "I just love getting birthday cards."

"You must have a lot," the boy said, climbing on a chair and leaning forward to watch Gert.

"Coffee's just about ready," Martha McIntosh announced. "Kate, do you want some too?"

Kate began unpacking one of the shopping bags. "Yes, thanks."

Dustin walked over to the table and took a seat. Trapped, that's what he was. A man surrounded by three generations of women determined to celebrate a birthday for as long as possible. He watched Kate pile gifts at Gert's feet, while Danny and Gert exclaimed over the mounting pile of presents.

"You're gonna open 'em now, right?" Danny asked.

"I sure am. And you can help me. You know where I keep the scissors," Gert said, and Danny scrambled off the chair and hurried across the room. He dug the scissors out of a drawer by the telephone and hurried back to Gert. "Thank you," she said, and cut a fistful of purple ribbons tied into a curly knot on top of a white box. "What do you suppose this is?"

Dustin glanced toward Kate, who looked as intrigued as Danny did. Her hair was lighter, though not as long as it was in high school. Her pink top and blue shorts showed off a figure that had only improved over the years. She looked as if she worked out in one of those fancy New York City gyms. He wondered if she had a lover, if they jogged together in Central Park and drank coffee in those restaurants with tables that lined the sidewalks.

''What do you take in it?''

Dustin turned as Martha set a cup of coffee in front of him.

''Just black, ma'am. Thank you.'' He hated himself for sounding like the hired help, but that's what he was. And that's the way Kate's mother eyed him. Did the woman know he'd made love to her daughter for one short summer so many years ago? Probably not, or she wouldn't have invited him to stay for coffee.

Cake appeared for everyone, plus a glass of milk for Danny, who watched as each present was unwrapped and exclaimed over. And the women were careful to include the boy in the impromptu party. How did women—some women—understand all of this, anyway? How did they know that a little boy had probably never been to a birthday gathering like this one? He sat back in his chair and sipped his coffee, despite that it burned his tongue. He ate cake—two pieces, even—and tried not to look at Kate too often.

She was still beautiful, of course. It was natural to be attracted to her, as he would be to any beautiful woman who smiled at Danny and made the boy feel part of things. He couldn't remember the last time he'd been with a woman, couldn't imagine anyone in Beauville he'd want in his bed. In his life.

And now here was Kate, the only woman he'd

ever loved. He'd been young and foolish, but he'd been in love just the same. And seeing her again could still tie his tongue in knots.

"It's time for bed, Danny," Dustin said, once the gifts were opened and the boy had stuffed all the wrapping paper in a garbage sack. Gert, frugal as ever, insisted on keeping the ribbons and bows, so Danny stuffed them into a deep drawer filled with string and assorted other things the woman figured she might need some day.

"Aww," the boy groaned. "Really?"

"Yep." Dustin scraped his chair back from the table and picked up his empty coffee cup to set in the sink. It was long past time to leave this house full of women and take the boy home to bed.

CHAPTER SIX

"MOTHER, ARE YOU sure you don't want to come back to town with us tonight?"

"I'm sure." Gert felt a little stiff after sitting at the kitchen table for so long, but she tried not to let on. Any complaint or sign of weakness would bring Martha down on her with that relentless worrying of hers. She shuffled into the sitting room, which used to be the dining room during the days when there were people to feed every day and night, and settled herself in her favorite overstuffed chair. "I like my own bed, Martha. You know I do."

"I know." Martha exchanged a look with Kate, who only smiled and sat down on the old maroon sofa.

"Your kitchen is all cleaned up, Gran," she said. "But I'll come out tomorrow and see what else you need to have done around here."

"It's your vacation, honey. You don't need to be working out here." But she knew Kate would come out anyway. The girl loved to clean, always had, but Gert had other plans for her granddaughter. If you wanted to write a book and your only granddaughter was a television writer, well, how lucky could an old lady be?

"I want to," she insisted. "You know I like to be out here. It's a chance to get the city out of my system."

"But your friends—"

"Will see plenty of me. I'm going to call Emily first thing tomorrow and see how she's doing. Make a cleaning list, Grandma, and I'll work my way through it."

"Cleaning. Now that's a good idea." Martha plopped on the couch and patted her daughter's knee. "Your grandmother has never been much for throwing things away and I'll bet there are some closets upstairs that could use a good going through."

"Closets," Gert muttered. "I don't care much about what's in those old closets. Tell me about the show, Kate. Is that nasty redheaded nurse going to kill someone else this week?"

Kate laughed. "I guess you've been watching the show. Lillian is a pretty frightening villain, isn't she?"

"You need a cowboy or two on that soap opera of yours, Katie." Her granddaughter hadn't fooled anyone with that I-hardly-know-Dustin-Jones attitude. Why, the young man could hardly take his eyes off her the entire time they were all in the kitchen eating cake. Gert watched Kate fidget with a crocheted pillow. "Have you ever thought of that? *Loves of Our Lives* could use some Texan men, to show those silly women in Apple Valley what real men are like."

"I'll see what I can do," Kate promised. "The head writer might be leaving, so there could be some changes. It's going to be a nerve-wracking summer on the show."

Changes. Gert wanted to tell her beloved Kate that changes were part of things, part of life. Of course, a woman could always dig in her heels and refuse to budge, or she could change right along with everything else. "How do you like my new ranch hands?"

"Hands?" Martha repeated. "You hired someone else?"

"The boy," Gert sighed. Her daughter didn't have much of a sense of humor, all things considered. Edwin sure had been funny, though, in his own way. She sure missed him, missed him teasing her about things. "Little Danny. Isn't he something?"

"Where do you think his mother is?" Kate asked, and Gert suspected there was more to her question than she was willing to let on.

"Dustin didn't say and I didn't ask. I think Dustin said Danny was going into third grade here in the fall," Gert mused, wishing she knew what was going on in that girl's head. "Why?"

"Just wondering."

"He sure likes cake." Martha looked at her watch. "We should let you get to bed, Mother. You've had quite a day."

"A good day," Gert reminded her, but truth to tell, she was tired. But she had a few more things to discuss with the girls before they left. "Did I tell you I'm writing a book?"

"About what?" Kate asked, sounding interested. Almost as interested as she'd been in Dustin's boy.

"About my life. Beauville. Texas. Everyone keeps telling me that I must have a lot of stories to tell."

"Oh, Lord," Martha moaned. "Whatever for?"

"I'd like to be rich before I die," her mother said. "And I sure would like to meet Katie Couric."

"What does Katie Couric have to do with the price of beans?"

"She's the cute little gal on TV."

"I know who she is, Mother. I want to know what she has to do with your writing a book."

Kate began to laugh. "Gran, do you want to be on television?"

Gert nodded. "I sure do."

"If you'd come to New York you could be an extra on the show."

"I'm not fancy enough for that, Katie. I want to be like those old women who were on TV a few days—or was it weeks—ago. They'd made themselves a bunch of money, just talking about their lives and giving advice."

"It's a good idea," her granddaughter declared. "I would think your stories would be very interesting."

"You can't even type." Martha hesitated. "Can you?"

"Enough. Maybe I'll get me a computer."

"A computer." Her lips pursed with disapproval.

"That's what I said, Martha. A computer. One of them little ones like Kate carries around. So I could put it on the kitchen table."

"I brought my laptop with me," Kate said. "I can teach you how to use it."

"Don't encourage her. The attic is already filled with scrapbooks and letters and heaven only knows what else. I suppose some things could be donated to the county historical society someday," Martha said, still unenthusiastic about book writing and television appearances.

"*Someday* meaning after I'm dead and buried?" Gert didn't like the idea of strangers looking through her personal letters, and there were a few secrets here and there that folks in town wouldn't like made public. Come to think of it, though, things like that might spice up the book a little bit. Make it more interesting than dust storms and recipes.

"I'm not sure writing a book guarantees you'll be on TV," Kate said, but she looked like she was enjoying the conversation. Gert bet the girl didn't do a lot of smiling in New York City. Too much stress, that's what everyone said about living in the city. The girl needed more clean air and good hearty food. "We'll have to go through those things upstairs. For ideas."

"I don't think that's such a good idea," Martha said, rising from the couch. "What's in the past should stay in the past."

"Why, Martha, are you so goldarned upset?"

"Mom?"

"I've had enough of this talk. And I don't think anyone should be writing anything about family secrets." Martha didn't look at either one of them. Instead she stalked out of the room.

"Gran didn't say anything about family secrets," Kate called after her. Gert could have told her that wouldn't work. When Martha was in one of her fusses, there was no talking her out of it. Sure enough, Martha returned to the living room and kissed Gert goodbye, but she didn't look happy.

"I wish you'd change your mind," Martha said.

"About writing a book?"

"About coming home with us."

"I'm staying here," Gert declared, "until I sell the place or the hearse comes to take me away."

"Gran," Kate said, making a face at her. "I'll be back in the morning, so have a list ready for me. That is, unless the hearse beats me out here."

Gert chuckled. "Go on, both of you. Thank you again for a lovely day." She took Kate's hand and whispered, "You won't forget to bring your computer tomorrow?"

"No. Go to bed."

"I will," she promised, wishing Martha wasn't leaving in such a snit. What secrets would her daughter want to keep private, anyway? Martha Knepper McIntosh had never done anything wrong in her life.

Unlike a lot of other folks around here.

"SHE REALLY SHOULDN'T stay out here alone anymore, should she?" Kate turned the car around and headed away from the ranch house. She drove slowly, reluctant to leave her grandmother on her own.

"No." Her mother sighed. "I've tried so hard to get her to move into town with me, but you know how stubborn she is. And she makes me feel ridiculous for worrying about her after we argue about it.''

''She loves that place.''

''Kate, honey, it hasn't always been a bed of roses out there for Gran.''

''Because?''

''Gran's first husband wasn't anything to shake a stick at.''

''Meaning?''

''Meaning I don't know how she did it. My father—Mother's second husband—ran the grocery store. We lived in town until my father retired.''

''And that's when they moved back to the ranch?''

''Yes. Your grandmother always ran the place, even when I was a little girl. We all spent weekends out there. She always was a really hard worker.''

''She's a very strong person,'' Kate said, wishing she had just one-tenth of that strength. Here she was, a twenty-seven-year-old woman in the prime of her life, and she felt ridiculously exhausted at the end of each day. ''Why are you upset about her writing her memoirs, Mom? Do we really *have* family secrets?''

''I guess I don't want everyone knowing our business,'' she said, but Kate wondered if there was more to it than that.

"But Gran's life is so unique, and she's lived so long."

"Long enough to know that you shouldn't go stirring up the past and making folks remember things."

"Remember things like what?"

Silence greeted that answer, so Kate tried again. "Was her first husband a criminal or something?"

"I am not going to discuss this with you, Kate."

Bingo. The first husband, Hal Johnson, must have done something very wrong. And Martha didn't want it rehashed, though he'd been dead long before Martha was born. Why would Martha be embarrassed by anything that Hal had done? It didn't make sense, but maybe Gran would explain it all.

"Okay," Kate said, then changed the subject. "Gran seems to be getting around pretty well, don't you think? And her mind is just as sharp as it ever was."

"I go out there every morning and every evening," Martha said, her voice breaking as if she was trying not to cry. "Or sometimes I come out and spend the afternoon. It would be so much easier if she would move into town. I worry so."

"What can I do to help? I know a week isn't much but—"

"Would you stay with your grandmother out at the ranch for a few days?

"Of course," Kate replied, glancing toward her mother. "Is that all?"

"It's a lot," she said. "Not that I don't want you at the house with me, but if you were there I wouldn't worry so much. And your grandmother listens to you. If *you* tell her she needs to move off of the ranch, she might just do it."

"I don't want to force her to leave the Lazy K, Mom." In fact, she couldn't picture her grandmother anywhere else but puttering around the old ranch house and wearing one of her faded print cotton dresses.

"None of us may have a choice much longer, Kate," her mother warned. "One fall, one false step…it scares me to think of all the things that could happen to her and no one would be there to help her."

"Dustin told me he doesn't live in the foreman's house because it's too far away from Gran. The bunkhouse is only a short walk from the main house."

"I didn't know that."

"I think he looks out for her," she said, picturing him hovering over her at the party. He was just as handsome as he ever was, she thought. More so, even. And the boy looked just like him. Each time she looked at him she remembered the pain she'd felt when she'd heard about Lisa Gallagher and her pregnancy. She shook off the memory. "Grandma loves having that little boy around."

"He seems nice enough. I imagine he reminds her of your uncle Hank at that age."

"No one ever really talks about Hank. What was he like?" Her mother's half brother had died several years before Martha married Ian McIntosh.

"Hank liked a good time," was all Martha would say. Before much longer they were driving past the crowded Steak Barn, then through town and onto Knight Street. Two blocks took them to "A Street," toward the two-story Victorian that had been Kate's home from the day she was born. Pale yellow with black shutters, it sat with other grand homes in the section of town referred to as "The Park," since its four blocks were a dead end, a self-contained area within the city.

The McIntosh house faced the park, with a view of grass, benches and a small play area for the local toddlers in the far northeast corner, across the street from what used to be the town's elementary school and now housed the Good Day Preschool.

"It's still so quiet here," Kate said, pulling the car into the driveway and parking in front of the garage. "Not like New York at all."

"Even Saturday nights aren't too wild in Beauville," Martha said, opening the car door. "My bed is sure going to feel good tonight."

"You must have worked so hard on the party. It was great."

"Thanks, honey. I'm lucky. How many people get to give their mother a ninetieth birthday party?" She smiled at Kate before stepping out of the car. "If you'll open the trunk I'll get the food out that needs to be refrigerated."

"I'll do it," Kate said. "Go on in and get the lights on." Her mother didn't argue, and instead went up the steps to the front porch. Soon the lights came on both inside and out, illuminating the tall windows and their lace curtains. A storybook house, Kate had always thought, filled with lovely polished silver and velvet-covered couches and gleaming cherry furniture. Her home had always smelled of furniture polish, not an unpleasant scent, but Kate had preferred the smell of hay and horses on her grandmother's ranch.

She didn't go inside right away. Instead she listened to the silence and became accustomed to a street devoid of taxis and traffic. Peaceful, Kate knew, unlike her life in the city. *Loves of Our Lives* was in turmoil, with a new director and executive producer. The writers had been told to come up with something spectacular for the November sweeps.

She thought of Gran's suggestion to bring in some Texas cowboys. Yes, the show needed a new hero.

Who didn't?

CHAPTER SEVEN

"I'D BE GLAD TO come with you." Kate watched her mother fuss over her hair in the hall mirror. They'd spent a hurried breakfast together and now her mother was rushing off to church.

"Honey, I would rather you spent the time with Gran. She'll be expecting you, you know. And aren't you supposed to stop in and see Emily?"

"Yes. But I could wait an hour or so."

"I'm off," her mother said, ignoring the offer. She picked up her purse and tucked a tissue inside.

"I'll pick something up for dinner," Kate offered. Her mother wore a fashionable navy linen dress that disguised her plump figure and made her seem younger than sixty-four years old. "I've never seen you wear that color before. You look nice."

"Well, thank you," she said, smiling. "I try. And don't worry about dinner. I'll meet you out at the ranch later on."

"Do you want me to pick you up?"

"I'll get a ride," she said, sounding more mysterious than a retired town clerk should sound.

"Okay." She watched her mother hurry out the front door as if she couldn't wait to get away. Usually when Kate was home she followed her everywhere. Kate would bet a week's salary that this had something to do with Carl Jackson, the romancing land developer. She couldn't picture her mother involved with any man, but the pudgy businessman who'd shaken her hand yesterday didn't look like someone her mother would fall for. And she couldn't envision her mother with anyone other than her sweet-tempered father, the quiet store owner with the patience of a saint. What on earth was the matter with the woman?

"So, WHAT DID I MISS at the birthday party?" Emily, her round face puffy from pregnancy, gave Kate a wicked grin. "Any romantic reunions? Unrequited longing? Lust? What?"

"Your hormone levels must be a mess," Kate told her, laughing as she sat across from Emily in her friend's tiny kitchen. George had taken the children to visit his mother for a while so Emily could get some rest. "Your imagination is just getting worse."

"Ha," she said, shifting in her chair so she could rest her legs on the seat of the chair next to hers. "You saw Dustin, right? And it's been eight—nine—years. And he's still as handsome as sin, isn't he?''

"Yes."

"As handsome as those New York actors you boss around?''

"Those New York actors are either married or gay," Kate said. "Maybe Dustin's married. He has a boy."

"Not married," Emily said. "George said." And if George said it, then it was fact. The man knew everything that went on in three counties. "So he's all yours for the taking."

"Oh, Em. I don't want him." She was no longer stupid, she hoped. Or gullible. She now knew that when a man said, "No commitments, no strings," he meant exactly what he said.

"I don't know about that. Some things don't change that much," Emily said, patting her belly. "Except for my stomach, which keeps getting bigger."

"How are you feeling?" she asked, grateful for the change in subject.

"Fine, unfortunately. I had false labor pains yesterday, which is why we missed the party. I knew it wasn't the real thing, but George made me go to bed and rest."

"You didn't miss much. A cake with candles blazing, my mother making eyes at Carl Jackson, Dustin's little boy getting his picture taken with my grandmother, Elizabeth and Jake looking happy and ready to be parents, Lorna Sheridan with a cute little baby." She took a sip of coffee. "I understand you all know each other."

"Lorna and Elizabeth are great," Emily said. "And eager recipients of all of my maternal advice. And I have a lot of advice."

"Do you have any for me?"

"Yes. Come home and make babies, too. Think of the fun we could have."

"Any other advice?"

"Make those teenagers on the show behave. That little blond gal—Becky?—needs to be grounded, or locked in her room." Emily looked over at the shopping bag Kate had brought with her. "Did you bring food?"

"Better than food," Kate declared, bending down to lift a gift-wrapped box out of the bag. "Saks."

"Be still my heart. And tell me it's something that doesn't have a waist."

"Would I do that to you? Open it." Every summer she brought her best friend something outrageously New York and chic, something meant to make Emily laugh. But this time Kate had opted for something less flamboyant. She watched as her friend ripped off the paper and lifted the lid of the dress box to reveal a buttercup yellow linen sundress.

"Oh, Kate, it's beautiful."

"Calf-length, machine washable, with buttons up the front. It's for after you have the baby." She helped move the wrappings away and shoved the paper into the shopping bag. Poor Emily could barely move. "And it doesn't have a waist, I promise. Waists aren't in this year."

"Thank goodness." She held it up and grinned. "I absolutely love it, Kate. You know redheads love yellow."

"If it doesn't fit I can exchange it when I get back, so hurry up and have the baby so you can try it on."

"I told George I'd take a long walk today, to get things going. Want to come?" She carefully folded the dress and tucked it back into the box.

"I can't. I'm heading out to the ranch."

Emily giggled. "Of course you are."

"To help my grandmother, Em, not to ogle the hired help."

"There are rumors she's going to sell him the place, you know."

"Rumors," Kate repeated. "That's all they are, because she hasn't said anything to me about selling." And selling was something her grandmother would never do. "The only thing she's told me is that she's writing a book."

"A book about what?"

Kate rose and, making herself at home at Emily's as she always had, refilled their coffee cups. "Her life, the story of the town. I'm not really sure, but she wants to meet Katie Couric and be on television."

Emily laughed. "If anyone can do it, it's Grandma Gert."

"My mother is having a fit. She thinks Gran is going to spill the family secrets."

"You mean she knows what you and Dustin were doing in the drive-in that summer?" Her belly went up and down as she laughed. "Now *that* would make interesting reading."

"I really hope you give birth to triplets."

"Unrequited lust must be making you a teeny bit vindictive," Emily said. "You'd better hurry up and get out to the ranch before I make you my birthing coach."

"Birthing coach?" she echoed. "Are you having contractions?"

"I will," Em promised, "if you keep making me laugh like this." She patted her belly and spoke as if talking to the child inside. "Don't mind Auntie Kate. She's never been able to resist a cowboy."

"I can resist," Kate promised. "I'm not going to be around long enough to get into trouble."

"We'll see," her friend said, smiling as if she knew exactly how flustered Kate felt whenever Dustin Jones was in the vicinity.

THE BOY GREETED her when Kate drove up in the yard. He clutched a dirty metal truck and gave her one of his shy smiles as she climbed out of the Lincoln. Oh, yes, she thought. His father all over again, and Kate willed herself to resist the kid's charm—which wasn't going to be easy, because he was staring up at her as if she was a goddess.

"Hi." It was surprisingly nice to be a goddess, even when it was this particular kid making her feel that way.

"Hi," Danny answered, falling into step beside her as she headed toward the kitchen door.

"How are you this morning?" she asked, wondering why she had an escort. She wasn't exactly sure what to say to him. She didn't really want to talk to the boy.

"Good."

"It's a nice day to play with your truck," Kate said, hesitating in front of the kitchen door. She wondered if he waited to be invited inside. She surprised herself by inviting him. "Did you want to come in?"

"Okay." He hurried to hold the door open for her, and Kate struggled to keep a straight face. He was so serious about being a gentleman, even though he was covered in a layer of Texas dust and had a cowlick sticking straight up from the back of his head. The truck came right into the kitchen with him.

"Grandma Gert," he called. "Guess who's here!"

Gran looked up from reading the newspaper and pretended to be surprised. "Well, my goodness! Kate and Danny have come to say good morning."

"I brought lunch, too," Kate said, crossing the kitchen to give her a hug. "Don't get up. Stay right there and I'll make a fresh pot of coffee for us." She turned to Danny. He may as well make himself useful. "Would you like to carry in the groceries? They're in the back of the car."

"Sure." He set the truck by the door and hurried off, the door banging shut behind him.

"I suppose you brought that fancy coffee again."

"I sure did." She leaned against the scratched Formica counter and surveyed the kitchen. Pine cupboards lined two walls, the refrigerator sat at the end of the south wall. She'd bet it could use a good scrubbing, since Gran was known for saving food long past its prime.

"You've got that look in your eyes, Katie. That cleaning look." Gert frowned at her. "I thought we would work on the book instead."

"We'll talk about it while I clean. How about that?" She rinsed out the coffeepot and filled it with cold water. "Do you want an early lunch or just coffee right now?"

"Coffee and cake sounds good." She shoved

the papers aside and stood. "I'll fix the cake. There's so much left over we could be eating it 'til Labor Day."

It was useless to argue with her. Useless to try to spoil her. Kate went to the door and held it open for Danny, who had somehow managed to carry four plastic bags in one trip.

"That's a lot of stuff," he said, dropping it on the old linoleum. Thank goodness she hadn't bought eggs. "You're gonna clean a whole lot, huh?"

"Yes, I sure am."

"Ladies like to do that, huh?"

"Some do," she said, picking up two of the bags and setting them on the counter. She found the electric grinder she'd purchased three years ago in the same cluttered cabinet where she'd left it, then opened the bag of coffee beans and proceeded to finish making coffee.

"Here, Danny," she heard Gran say. "I saved the comics for you." She turned to see the little boy seat himself at the table as if he did so every day. And maybe he did. Gran reached over to smooth his hair, then set a plastic plate filled with cake slices on the table. "Where's your father this morning?"

"Cleanin' the barn, I think."

"Oh, dear," her grandmother said.

"What's the matter?"

"Dustin should be taking the day off. It's the only time he gets off, except for Saturday afternoons."

Danny shrugged. "We're gonna go to town later."

"Does he know where you are?"

The boy shrugged again and Gert answered for him. "Danny's allowed to play between his house and my house, Kate. His daddy will know where to find him."

A ninety-year-old woman and a little boy certainly seemed to have everything under control.

"I froze cinnamon rolls," Gran announced. "You could heat 'em up for your coffee, put 'em in that microwave oven you gave me, if you're tired of birthday cake."

Her mouth watered at the thought. "I guess cleaning can wait."

"Grandma Gert makes good stuff," the boy declared before he returned to the comics spread out in front of him.

"Yes, I know." She wondered how much time the boy spent at the house. He certainly seemed comfortable, which bothered her a little.

"Is your fancy coffee ready yet? It sure smells good."

"Almost," she said, glancing out the window at the barn. Someone had begun painting it white, which she hadn't noticed last night. "You're painting the barn?"

"Dustin's idea," Gran said. "We're sprucing the place up."

"That's nice."

"And about time, too. This ranch is a hard place to keep up," Gran said. "Needs a young man."

"You've done fine so far," Kate reminded her.

"Ha! Take a good look around, honey, and you'll see all sorts of things I've had to let go." She shook her head. "I hate letting the ranch get in this condition. Sometimes I look around and figure your mother is right, and it's time to let someone else take over."

"But—"

"Pour me some of that coffee, Katie," her grandmother said, changing the subject as if it was too painful for her. "My mouth is watering."

Later, after the three of them had eaten their fill of birthday cake and cinnamon rolls dripping with butter, Kate refilled her coffee cup and began lining up cleaning supplies on the counter.

"You don't have to do this," Gran said, stifling a yawn.

"You don't have any choice," Kate said, giving her a smile as she unwrapped a new sponge. "Go take a nap, or watch television."

"Can I stay, too?" Danny brought his empty juice glass to the sink.

"I think we'd better let Grandma Gert take a rest now," Kate told him, wondering just exactly how much time the child spent here. Was Dustin using Gran as a baby-sitting service? That was another thing she would have to look out for.

"We were going to talk about the book," Gert said, clearing the table and coming over to set the dirty dishes in the sink. "I've been thinking how to start it, earlier than when I was born."

"Before 1910?"

"My father told me stories," she said.

"Stories?" Danny picked up his truck and tucked it under his arm. "What kind of stories?"

"Oh, about his father and mother, and their parents," Gert said. "Does your daddy tell you stories?"

"No." The boy frowned. "We don't have any family."

Kate and Gert exchanged a look over the boy's head, then Gert patted his shoulder. "I'll tell you a story next time you come over to visit," she promised.

"Okay." With that, he started out the door, but hesitated before he left. "Thank you for the breakfast, um, lunch," he called.

"You're welcome," Kate said, watching him walk across the dusty yard. His serious expression reminded her of his father. *We don't have any family*. Was Dustin estranged from his brothers? She could see why, especially when it came to the one who was in jail. But what of Danny's mother's family?

"There's more to that story," Gran said, shaking her head. "Those two seem all alone in the world."

"I wonder why."

"Dustin doesn't talk much," her grandmother said. "But I guess you know that."

"He never did like to talk about his family," she agreed.

"So you were good friends?"

"For a while," she admitted, avoiding Gran's gaze. "Kid stuff."

"Kid stuff," Gert repeated. "Is that the same as 'puppy love?'"

"I guess." If puppy love meant making love in the back seat of a car twenty or thirty times.

"He's a handsome man," her grandmother said. "Reminds me of your grandfather at that age, tall and strong. You haven't met anyone like that in New York City, I'll bet."

"No." And Kate didn't know why, except that the few relationships she'd had were surprisingly disappointing in the passion department. And yet none of those men—an accountant, an actor and one brilliant associate producer—had broken her heart.

Gran left the table and disappeared into the parlor for a moment. When she returned she held an armload of papers. "I've made some notes."

"You've started already?"

"Oh, yes, dear. At my age it's too risky to put anything off 'til tomorrow." She seated herself at the kitchen table and pointed to the chair across from her. "All this cleaning can wait, dear. Should I start with when I was born or should I start with my grandfather's life?"

"Well, you can do it either way," she said, sitting down and eyeing the large stack of papers. Gran's handwriting, fine and elegant, covered the pages. There were documents, too, yellowed papers with official seals peeking out of the untidy stack. "We can call it a 'rough draft' and then rewrite it any way you think is best. What's important is to get it all down."

"Get it all down," Gran repeated, "in a rough draft." She nodded. "I like that 'rough draft' business. It sounds very professional. Did you bring your computer?"

"It's in the car."

"Well, go get it, Kate, and we'll get started. I'm not going to live forever, you know."

CHAPTER EIGHT

"ASK DUSTIN IF HE could carry those trunks down for us," Gert said, leaning back in her favorite overstuffed armchair. "He won't mind."

"It's his day off," Kate reminded her. "Danny said they were going to town."

"They haven't left yet." Gert could see everything from this chair, including the view from the front windows that showed everyone coming and going along the ranch road. She'd kept a careful eye out for the young man's truck and so far she knew he hadn't gone anywhere at all.

"I can get them," Kate assured her, stacking another pile of papers into a neat bundle. They'd been organizing Gert's papers for a couple of hours, but there was a lot more to do and Gert knew darn well that Kate couldn't move those heavy trunks downstairs all by herself. "I can leave the trunks where they are and just bring down what's in them."

"It'll take too long. And those things could fall apart in your hands," she warned.

"I can figure it out," the girl assured her.

"Suit yourself," Gert said, trying not to smile at the stubborn streak that Kate inherited from her side of the family. How else could anyone stay ranching in Texas for a hundred and fifty years if they didn't have a hard head and a wagon load of determination? "But I'd better come with you, then, to help."

Kate looked horrified, as expected. "Gran, stay right here. I'll manage."

"Nope." She struggled out of her chair. Her darn legs were always stiff after sitting down for a couple of hours, but it didn't last long. "I'll be fine once I get myself going again."

"Never mind," her granddaughter said, hurrying over to the chair to help Gert sit back down again. "I'll get Dustin."

"Well," she drawled, "if you're sure..."

"I'll be back in a few minutes," Kate assured her. "Just stay put."

Oh, she'd stay put, all right. For now. She'd sent her beautiful granddaughter off to find a cowboy. A good man, that Dustin. A hard worker, too. Didn't shirk from dirty work, either. And knew a lot about ranching. Taking care of the boy the way he did showed he was the kind of man a woman wanted around, the sort of man who took his responsibilities seriously.

And Kate needed a man in her life. And Gert

needed a man to take over this ranch. She used to think she'd leave it to Kate and Jake. It was a big enough spread for the both of them and they were smart enough to figure out how to work it out, not that either one of them needed the place. But Kate seemed content to live in that darn city and Jake already had his own place, a nice piece of land given to him by his boss, God rest his soul. R. J. Calhoun had been quite a man.

So she was free to do what she wanted with the Lazy K. She could "get creative," her lawyer had said the last time he was out here for coffee and cinnamon buns. He'd wiped his fingers and licked the frosting from his lips and then given her some advice she thought she just might take after all.

There was a lot to think about these days, but Gert surveyed her home and figured she had a little more time to figure out what was best. Dustin would make a good partner and he was the kind of man her Edwin would have liked.

Then again, Edwin liked just about everybody—except Hank, of course. Hank had always been difficult.

His sister, Martha, was nothing like him; she'd always aimed to do the right thing. And her granddaughter was her mother's child all the way. It was a treat to have Kate home, but it wouldn't be for long. And Dustin was here indefinitely. The man would make a good partner—for the ranch and for a woman, all right. If she could only get Kate to realize it before it was too late.

"My, my," she said aloud, used to talking to herself. "This could get interesting."

"I HATE TO BOTHER you, but—" Kate hesitated, standing in the wide doorway of the barn. The odor of sweet hay assaulted her as the breeze blew through the open doors, and Kate wished she had time to saddle one of the horses and take a long ride along the southern fence line. Later, she promised herself. When Gran took her afternoon rest, she would defy the heat for just a short while.

"But?"

"We—Gert needs your help moving some trunks from the attic and she wondered if you'd mind—"

"I don't mind," he said, those dark eyes looking her over as if he didn't like what he saw. He leaned the hay rake in the corner and pulled off his thick work gloves. "That's what she pays me for."

"She said it was your day off."

He shrugged, as if days off didn't matter. As if he had all the time in the world, which Kate found faintly annoying. No one should look as good as this man, all dust-covered denim and tanned skin. He took off his Stetson and banged the dust off it before replacing it on his head.

"Where's Danny?"

"He should be around the back of the barn. He's got a digging operation going."

"Oh." She fell into step beside him. "He showed me his truck." Odd that they should be talking about the child whose conception had broken her teenage heart.

"It's his favorite toy," Dustin said. "It was the only thing he had when he moved—" He stopped, as if he hadn't meant to say as much as he had.

"When he moved in with you?"

He nodded. "Yeah. A few months ago."

"Where's his mother?"

"Beats the hell out of me."

She hadn't expected that particular answer. Dustin reached the corner of the barn and called to the boy, telling him he'd be over at Gert's for a few minutes. Danny waved, his smile widening as he spotted Kate, but he didn't seem interested in following them this time. She supposed he'd eaten enough cinnamon rolls and pieces of cake to be content for an hour or two.

"Will he be all right out here alone?"

"He knows to stay right there," he said, but he glanced back at the boy as if to make sure Danny was occupied with his trucks. "He's a good kid."

"Gran likes him."

"She's good to him," he said. "He needs—" and then he stopped whatever it was he was going to say.

"Needs what?" she prompted, wishing he wouldn't walk so fast. She'd forgotten that about him.

"A grandmother, I guess," was his reluctant response. "He gets lonely around here, just hanging out with me."

"He doesn't look unhappy," she said, glancing back over her shoulder at the small boy playing in the mud hole. "In fact, he looks like he's doing exactly what a boy his age should do, don't you think?"

Dustin turned, and his frown deepened before he headed toward the house again. "Yeah. Sure." But he didn't sound convinced.

"You're painting the barn."

"Yeah."

"Why?"

"It needs it."

"What else do you do around here? Gran doesn't keep much stock anymore."

"We're running some cattle now. And we're training some of the younger horses, the ones with potential, to sell."

"Whose idea was that?"

"Mine." He stopped and looked down at her. "You got a problem with that?"

"Maybe."

"And this is your business because...?"

"Because she's my grandmother."

"And she's going to be my partner," he said, those dark eyes holding her gaze. Oh, handsome as sin, that was Dustin, especially when he was holding his temper—or trying to.

"Partner?" she echoed. "Since when?"

"Since she suggested it." He'd stopped, crossed his arms over his chest and planted his booted feet firmly on the ground. Almost as if he was daring her to try to knock him down.

"You've bought into this place?"

"The cattle operation, yes. The horses, yes. The land? Not yet."

"She'd never sell any part of the Lazy K."

"Maybe," he said, one corner of his mouth tilting into the faintest suggestion of a smile. "Maybe not. You don't want this place, so why are you getting mad?"

"I'm not mad and I've never said I don't want this ranch." She fought the urge to give his chest a shove, just on the off chance that he would topple backward into the dirt.

One eyebrow rose and he still wore that mocking expression. "So that's why you moved to New York and only come back once a year. You really love ranching, I guess."

It was twice a year, but even that sounded pathetic, so Kate kept her mouth shut as Dustin continued. "And when you come back to Texas to stroll around in your designer jeans and your expensive snakeskin boots you manage to put in fifteen hour days getting the place squared away?"

"Do I sense some animosity?"

He smiled then, a full charming smile that made her blink as she looked up into his face. "No, sweetheart. I don't have time for animosity. I've got a ranch to run."

"Yes," she said, hoping she sounded sickeningly sweet. "That's what you're getting paid for, isn't it."

"Yes, ma'am," he said, all exaggerated politeness. "Now get your sweet little ass out of my way."

Kate stepped aside. Dustin Jones wasn't anywhere near as nice as he had been nine years ago. "You've changed," she muttered.

"Yeah."

"I suppose we both have."

"Nine years is a long time," he said, as they reached the house and he opened the kitchen door for her. "A lot changes."

"For instance?"

"Well, for one thing, we just spent five minutes together and kept our clothes on."

Kate let out a surprised laugh. "You're right," she said, hoping the heat she felt on her face didn't show. "I'd forgotten—"

"No, you haven't," he said, following her into the kitchen. "You're blushing."

"It's the heat," she said, fanning her face with her hand as if there were a remote chance that would cool her skin. "I'll fix us something cold to drink. Water, iced tea, coffee?"

"Ice water's fine," he said, stepping through the kitchen to stand in the doorway of the parlor. "Geez, Gert, what are you doing?"

"Working on my book. Kate's going to teach me how to use her computer and I'm going to get rich."

"Sounds like a plan," he agreed. "Where are those trunks you want moved?"

"In the attic. Once you're on the second floor, you'll see a door opposite the bathroom. That's the attic. You think you can carry them yourself?"

"If I can't I'll come back down and get Kate," he assured her, and Kate heard his footsteps on the stairs as she set iced drinks on the kitchen table.

"He's a good man," Gran said, looking pointedly at her granddaughter. "A woman could do a lot worse, and believe me, I know what I'm talking about."

"Your first husband, you mean?"

"He was a drinker. Never grew up. I think the war had a lot to do with it. Or that's the excuse I've given him all these years." She picked up a black-and-white photograph and handed it to Kate. "Our wedding day. Don't we look young, Mr. and Mrs. Hal Johnson?"

Kate studied the photo, especially her grand-mother's unlined face. Her hair was pulled back under a wide-brimmed hat, her dress was floaty and ankle-length. "How old were you?"

"Just seventeen. My parents were furious, but there wasn't anything they could do."

"Why? Did you elope?"

"We did," Gert agreed, "but I was two months' pregnant at the time. Anything less than marriage would have caused a great scandal, and my parents didn't approve of scandals."

"I never knew you had to get married," Kate said, studying Hal Johnson's square face. His ex-pression was defiant and proud as he held his wife's arm.

"You think your generation invented sex?"

"Of course not, though we did put it on televi-sion," Kate admitted, chuckling. "Are you putting that in your book, too?"

"I haven't decided yet. I suppose I should."

"That's up to you." And perhaps why her mother was against this "story of my life" project. "Does Mom know?"

Gert shrugged. "I haven't a clue, Katie. She didn't think much of Hank, not that I blamed her. He was a hard boy to like sometimes, so wild and full of the dickens."

Dustin appeared on the stairs, an old brown trunk in his arms. "Where do you want this?"

"Set it down anywhere," Gert said, indicating a floor covered in papers.

"Maybe under the window?" Kate suggested, wondering how much that trunk weighed. Dustin carried it easily, but then again he was used to hay bales.

"Who were you talking about?" He set the trunk down and fiddled with the padlock until it fell open.

"Mom's half brother," Kate said. "Hank Johnson."

Dustin lifted the lid of the trunk. "Jake's father?"

"And my son," Gert said. "Though he wasn't much to be proud of. He had too much of his father in him, I suppose. I divorced Hal in 1930—write that down, will you, Kate?—which was a big scandal in those days."

"I'll bet." Dustin sneezed. "You must have kept the Beauville gossips busy."

"Bless you," the old woman said. "And yes, the old folks were scandalized. My mother swore she'd never get over the shame of it all."

"Do you want the other trunks down here, too? I think there are three more." He put his hands on his narrow hips, the typical pose of a man waiting for instructions. He stood there patiently, his shoulders impossibly wide, his jeans snug on his long legs. His look of innocence didn't fool Kate. He was the same person who had once ripped off the buttons on her best blouse.

"As long as you're here…" Gert said, leaning over to poke at the contents of the trunk. "I think these are some of the ranch account books. Looks like my father's writing. Go with him, Kate. See if you can find any more photo albums. After the divorce I put a lot of things up in the attic."

Wonderful. She would be in a dimly lit, stuffy attic, alone with a man who'd reminded her that they'd had a, um, physical relationship at one time. A *long* time ago, she told herself, feeling awkward and uncomfortable, amazingly like the way she'd felt the first time she'd gone out with him.

She stepped outside of the refreshment building at the drive-in, her popcorn and soda pop purchased after waiting in a long line of silly junior high kids, only to discover in the growing darkness that her friends had left her. Emily wasn't with them tonight—she was working late at the grocery store and then George was picking her up—so she wasn't there to give her a ride home.

"Hey," Dusty Jones said, from the open window of a banged-up Buick sedan. He was certainly handsome, with a reputation for wildness, though he'd never seemed anything but quiet in the English class they'd shared during her junior year, or the history class when they were seniors. She had never talked to him outside of school before.

The Jones boys were the kind that fathers wouldn't permit to hang around their daughters, but right now Dustin looked pretty safe to Kate, safer than standing all alone in the empty space where Patti Lou's station wagon had been parked.

"Hey," she answered, trying to sound sophisticated yet knowing her only option now was to call her father for a ride.

"Your friends left ten minutes ago," Dusty said. "They were in a big hurry."

"Great," Kate said, disgusted with herself for hanging out with a group of cheerleaders. Emily had tried to warn her, but Kate really wanted to see this movie and couldn't bear the thought of another Friday night at home watching television with her parents.

"Get in," Dustin said, and she watched as he leaned over and opened the passenger door. "Before the bugs get you."

She did, of course, with her popcorn and drink balanced carefully so she wouldn't spill on the seat of his car. He took the drink from her fingers and put it in the cup holder by the dashboard. "There," he said. "You might as well stay and watch the movie."

"What about your date?"

He shrugged. "I guess you're it."

"Oh." Now that was stranger than Patti Lou driving off and leaving her stuck. Every girl Kate

*knew thought he was the most handsome boy in
the class, though he kept to himself pretty much
and dated some of the wilder girls in the county.
Why would he want to be nice to her, the brainy
geek with small breasts?*

"Or," he said, looking at her with something
she swore was disappointment. *"I could drive you
home."*

*And miss out on something exciting to tell Emily
tomorrow? No way. She wanted to see this movie.
And she didn't want to go home.*

*She held out the box of popcorn toward him.
"Want some?"*

"What?" Dustin turned around and looked
down at her as she climbed the last of the stairs.

"I didn't say anything."

"I thought you did." He gave her an odd look
and then turned around and headed toward another
trunk. "Maybe you were just panting."

"I wasn't panting. I walk three miles a day."

"Groaning, then."

She ignored him. The attic looked almost exactly the same as she remembered it from fifteen
or twenty years ago. A treasure trove of family
paraphernalia, it was an antique-lover's dream.
Chairs, tables, boxes and odd containers were jum-
bled together against the outer walls, though the
piles weren't as high farther away from the door.
Gran must have dumped things she didn't want to

throw away just inside the door. A few dusty paths wound through the mess, and a streak of painted brown floor showed where Dustin had dragged the trunk to where he could lift it.

"I guess it doesn't matter which one," he said, bending toward another dust-covered trunk. "I wonder how long this stuff has been up here."

"I don't think they threw anything out, do you?"

"You come from a long line of pack rats."

"It does run in the family," she confessed, thinking of her closet in the Apple Street house. "If my mother really does move into those retirement villas, I'm in deep trouble. What about you?"

"Our family didn't have much of anything to begin with, never mind anything worth saving for thirty or forty years." He started dragging the trunk toward the door, so Kate moved some boxes aside to give him more room. She backed into something hard and heavy that fell sideways, toward Dustin's shoulder.

They both grabbed the ironing board at the same time, which sent the trunk thudding to the floor. Kate's fingers ended up underneath Dustin's as they prevented the board from falling. His hand was very warm, she noticed, wondering how to move away without dropping the old wooden board on his head. And when she looked up at him, his gaze was on her mouth, and then her eyes.

He looked as surprised as she felt, Kate realized, unable to move. He was very close. Too close, or maybe not close enough, she thought. The muscles in his jaw tightened, as if he was trying to control his temper. And then he said, "Let go. I've got it."

He shifted his hand, breaking contact. And he looked away, stabilized the ironing board against the wall, and then he bent over to grab the handle of the trunk again.

"Katie?"

"Yes?" She'd forgotten how dark his eyes were, forgotten the dimple in his chin and the way his voice dipped lower when he spoke to her.

"You have to get out of the way."

"Sure." Kate climbed onto an old stool and let him haul the trunk toward the attic door.

She hated feeling like this. She was a successful television writer. She'd graduated from NYU, wrangled an internship with *Loves of Our Lives,* and made herself indispensable when her boss needed advice from "a younger generation." She'd worked her way up from assistant to the assistant producer to one of the staff writers on a daytime soap that was consistently ranked in fourth place in the ratings. They'd even been bumped up to third for one two-week period, during the culmination of a story line that Kate had helped develop. She lived alone in a trendy apartment, knew her way around New York well enough to give the taxi drivers directions, had friends on three continents and attended the daytime Emmy awards four years in a row. She went to parties with her friends from the show and got her facials at Elizabeth Arden.

She didn't need sex with Dustin Jones, too.

CHAPTER NINE

HE DIDN'T HAVE time for this. Didn't have extra
hours for emptying an attic and digging through
old papers. Gert was one hell of a fine old woman,
and she and her granddaughter could spend their
days messing around with Texas history, but he
had a ranch to run. He had a ranch to *build*. Just
the thought of making something for himself and
Danny made him want to work twenty-four hours
a day.

"What do you think?" Gert was asking, looking
across the room at him while he took one step
backward, closer to the kitchen and freedom.
"Should I start with the town's beginnings or
should I start from the present—me at ninety—and
work back?"

"Flashbacks," Kate mused, sitting cross-legged
on the floor while she emptied a trunk. "That
could be interesting."

"Well," Dustin said, moving another step closer
to the kitchen. "I guess you could do it either way,
Gert. I don't think it matters a whole lot." He was

a rancher, not a writer, for God's sake. And he didn't want to be within touching distance of Kate McIntosh. He'd gone down that road once and it had cost him.

"It matters," the old woman said. "Kate says I have to 'hook the reader.'"

"Oh." He resettled his hat on his head. "I'd better check on Danny."

"He's coming toward the back door now," Gert said. "I can see him from this chair." Dustin turned and, sure enough, the boy was just about to knock on the door. "That's why I like this chair the way it is," Gert added. "I can see just about everything that goes on, from who's coming up the road to who's coming to the door. It's a pretty good view of the world when your feet hurt."

Kate looked up. "Do your feet hurt?"

"Honey, everyone's feet hurt once in a while. Dustin?" She looked at him and Dustin could swear her eyes twinkled. The old lady was enjoying this. "Your feet hurt?"

"Yes, ma'am," he said. "Sometimes they do."

"I like a good foot rub," Gert declared. "My second husband was sure good at that." She raised her voice. "Come on in, Danny!"

The boy didn't need to be told twice. Dustin watched the kid hurry toward them. He'd left the truck outside the way Dustin had told him, which was good. He was catching on to all sorts of things:

manners, conversation, chewing with his mouth closed and remembering to flush. His mother hadn't spent much time teaching him the basics; she couldn't raise a kid and drink herself into a stupor at the same time.

"Did you wipe your feet?"

"Yep." Danny smiled up at him, one of those rare smiles that made Dustin wonder how the boy had survived living with Lisa and her assorted boyfriends. "I sure did. There was mud and everything." He looked past his father to Gert. "Wow, you've made a mess."

"We're working on my book," Gert told him. "I'm telling my stories to Kate and she's going to type them into her computer for me."

"Cool."

"Well," Dustin said, putting his hand on the boy's shoulder to keep him from entering the room, "if there's nothing else to carry, we should get going."

"You could help sort." Gert pointed to an unopened trunk. "We're dividing things by decades."

"Decades?" Danny frowned. "I don't know much about 'decades.'"

"That means every ten years," Kate said, giving the child the kind of smile that Dustin had taken for granted nine years ago. "Like 1970s, 1980s…"

"1960s?" he asked. "We learned that in school."

"I didn't like the sixties much," Gert said. "I can't say that was my favorite time, except for Martha's wedding. Now *that* was a nice day."

"That was in 1969, right?" Kate rifled through the stack of papers on her lap. "I think I have some of those ranch records here. I could tell you the price of beef in August 1969."

"Doesn't matter," her grandmother said. "No one wants to know about business. They'll want the human interest stuff. That's what they'll want to talk about on the *Today* show. I'm going to have to write about your uncle Hank, and my first husband, and what it was like to grow up without cars and toilets and CNN." She shook her head and looked over to Dustin. "My grandfathers were some of the first men to ranch this territory, you know."

Now there was something interesting. In spite of all the things he had to do, Dustin found himself curious. "You're related to R. J. Calhoun somehow, aren't you?"

"Oh," Gert said, those blue eyes twinkling at him. "The Calhouns. Now there's a story for you."

"Wait," Kate said, leaning over to grab her laptop computer. "Let me type while you talk."

Dustin released the boy, who tiptoed through the

piles of papers and sat at Gert's feet. Dustin leaned
in the doorway, content to stay on the opposite side
of the room from Kate. She looked too good, even
if she was a little too thin and too pale. He liked
his women robust, blond and holding a beer. Of
course, since he'd become a father there hadn't
been any women at all, robust or otherwise. The
Last Chance Saloon was off-limits, as were late
nights and female companionship. Maybe that's
why Kate unnerved him the way she did. Just
touching her hands sent him into thoughts of bed-
ding her. Several times. In a split second of mad-
ness, he'd wanted to lift her onto one of those old
chairs, spread her legs and take her right then and
there.

He had to get a grip.

"I've got work to do," he muttered.

"I thought you got the barn all cleaned up,
Dad," the boy said. "You said you were done."

"Yeah," he said, realizing that fathers didn't
have any privacy. "But there's always something
to do around here, and I have plenty of barn left
to paint whenever I run out of chores."

"It's too hot," Gert said. "Kate fixed you a nice
glass of ice water. It's there on the table behind
you." Dustin had no choice but to turn around and
pick up the glass. He took a few swallows of water
and cleared the dust from his throat while he tried
to think up a way to get out of this house and away

from Kate. He wished like hell she would go back to New York and leave him alone.

He hadn't thought of her much these past years, except once in a while. Like when he passed the Good Night Drive-In on his way to Marysville. Once or twice he'd awakened next to a woman whose name he couldn't remember and he wondered—just a few times—what it would have been like to wake up next to Kate. She'd been eighteen; there had been no beds in their summer romance.

"Dustin?"

He jerked back to attention. "What?"

"I said you shouldn't be working in this heat."

"Not a problem, Gert. Really." He smiled at her. "I know what I'm doing. Thanks for the water. Danny? Come on, it's time we were on our way."

"He can stay," Gert said. "Come back for dinner. We're eating at four."

"Thanks, Gert, but we're all set." He ignored the disappointed expression on the boy's face as Danny stood up and crossed the room. "We'll see you tomorrow morning, unless you need me before that."

And that, he figured, leaving the house, was that. All he had to do was keep his mind off work and his body away from Kate's. Two weeks was all.

Not much could happen in two weeks.

"WOULD YOU LIKE a beer, Carl?" Gert opened the refrigerator and pulled out a bottle. "We've got an extra."

"It's Sunday, Mother," Martha said, hurrying over to return the beer to the refrigerator and shut the door. "And it's not your beer, remember?"

"I borrowed a couple from my foreman," her mother explained, looking entirely too pleased with herself, "for my birthday."

"Thank you, Mrs. Knepper, but I'll take a rain check on the beer. Your foreman, is that one of the Jones brothers?"

"Dustin," Martha said.

"Those boys sure had their share of trouble," Carl said, looking every inch the successful Texas gentleman in his beige suit. Martha especially liked the turquoise and silver bolero at his collar. "That party was quite a celebration. There should be some good pictures in the newspaper tomorrow."

"I hope they got my good side," Gert said, winking at him as she walked past them into the parlor. Or what used to be the parlor. The room was filled with trunks, papers, boxes and some opened maps. It looked as if her mother had dumped the contents of her closet into the middle of the room.

"Mother, what are you doing?"

"Research," was the reply, "for my book."

"You're writing a book?" Carl looked intrigued.

Martha was real sorry she'd let Carl bring her here. She'd thought they might take a drive to Marysville after lunch, but Carl wouldn't hear of her missing a minute more of her daughter's visit home. She suspected he might be a little starstruck over Kate's job since he'd just started talking about making television commercials for the villas. "How about some iced tea, Carl?"

"Excellent, Martha, excellent," he said, rubbing his hands together as if he couldn't wait. That's what she liked about him. Enthusiasm. A willingness to do interesting things.

"Coming right up," she said. "Mother, what about you?"

"I'm having coffee right now. Kate brewed us a fresh pot."

"And where is Kate?"

"Back up in the attic," her mother said, "looking for old yearbooks."

"Yearbooks," Martha echoed. "Whatever for?"

"Because she thought she'd like to see what people looked like, so she could help me write about them better."

"I don't think you should write about them at all," she declared, getting out the good glasses from above the stove. They looked a little dusty, so she gave them a good rinse before filling them with ice cubes. She really should ignore her mother and come down and clean out these cupboards one of these days. "Why stir up trouble?"

"Trouble?" Carl shook his head and made himself comfortable in a kitchen chair. "It's history, Martha. And who better to tell it than the oldest woman in town?"

"I'd like to think I have more to recommend me than my ninety years, Carl," Gert sniffed. "Like my steel-trap memory and my scintillating storytelling ability."

"Well, yes, but—"

"I'm going to call it *My Beauville—A Woman Remembers*."

"Hmm," Carl said. "Sounds literary."

"Is that good or bad?"

"Well, I guess it could be either, but—"

"Ridiculous," was all Martha could think to say. "No one's going to want to read about Beauville. We're boring."

"No, we're not," her mother said. "We've had range wars and droughts, war heroes and love stories, buried treasure and mysterious deaths—all the things that make good reading."

"Scandals, too," Carl said. "We've had our share of scandals. Remember when that body was found out by the river? And the time the sheriff's deputy got shot and no one ever found out who did it? Old Bishop went to his grave not telling anyone the true story.''

"He was messing around on his wife," Martha said. "I think she shot him and he was too embarrassed to tell. Besides, she only took his big toe off.''

"I think she was aiming higher." Gert chuckled.

"Mother, please," Martha begged, handing Carl his drink.

"I should put that story in," the old woman muttered. She fished around the seat cushion and pulled out a pen. "I think that was in the 1970s." She scribbled something on a legal pad, ripped off the page and handed it to Carl. "Put that on the pile next to your feet, Carl. Last time I looked that pile was the seventies.''

"Sure." He did as he was told and took a sip of his iced tea. "I must say, Mrs. Knepper, you have quite a collection of historical information arranged here. Are you getting ready to move?''

"The Lazy K isn't for sale," Gert declared. "Dustin and I are going back in the cattle business.''

"The cattle business," Martha groaned. "Good Lord.''

"I think it's nice your mother still keeps active," the man said. "Writing books and raising cattle at her age is remarkable.''

She'd show him remarkable, Martha thought, if

she could get him alone and out of that nicely pressed suit. Nine years without sex was starting to make her cranky. She was getting more lines around her face and she worried that the insides of her body had dried up and disappeared from disuse.

Menopause hadn't fazed her, but loneliness and boredom were about to do her in.

"TAKE SOME OF THAT over to Jake's," Gert said, pointing to the oven-fried chicken breasts left in the pan. "I imagine Elizabeth isn't doing much cooking these days, poor thing."

"All right. I'll do it on my way home." Kate set one aside on a plate and covered it with plastic wrap. "I'm leaving you one for lunch tomorrow, or in case you get hungry later."

"I don't eat much," Gran confessed. "Gives your mother fits, but that's the way it is."

"Is she serious about Carl, do you think?" She put the rest of the chicken on one of Gran's scarred plastic dinner plates and wrapped it tightly with plastic wrap. Her mother had accepted a ride home from the real estate king instead of staying for dinner, which suited everyone. Gert wanted to talk about her book and Kate hoped to avoid any more scenes of her mother making eyes at Carl Jackson. What on earth was wrong with the woman?

"Hard to tell, but I wouldn't be surprised."

Gran turned on the hot water and squirted dish detergent into the sink. "Your father's been gone nine years now. Maybe she's looking for a new husband. A woman gets lonely."

"She'd be better off getting a dog."

"Now, Kate," her grandmother said in that warning tone Kate had heard many times before. "You can't expect your mother to live alone in that fancy house for the rest of her life."

"Yes, I can," she said, but she laughed at herself. "I depend on her—and you—to stay the same. It's comforting to know that the two people I love most in the world are right here—you here on the ranch making cinnamon rolls and Mom fussing over the dust on the mahogany banister. I can't picture anything else."

"That's plain ridiculous. Round up the silverware and toss it in here." She squeezed the water out of a sponge and wiped off a section of the counter closest to her, then spread a clean flour sack towel over it. "Things change."

Kate did as she was told and stacked the remaining dishes next to the sink. "People don't."

Gran gave her a sharp look and then turned her attention back to dishwashing. "Sometimes they do and sometimes they don't. That's what keeps life interesting. What about you? Is there a man there in New York who makes your heart beat fast when you look at him?"

"Not right now."

"It's time you started looking, you know," Gran said. "You're not getting any younger and it's time you settled down and started having a family."

"Yes, ma'am," Kate said, knowing full well her job and lifestyle wouldn't include a husband and babies any time soon. "I'll do my best."

"You should marry a Western man," Gran mused. "They don't come any finer." She frowned to herself and rinsed the silverware under the running water. "Most of 'em, anyway."

CHAPTER TEN

SHE'D FORGOTTEN about the yearbooks—those black-and-white photographs of the class of '55, the autographs, the recounting of dances and football games. Martha thumbed through the musty-smelling pages of the *Beauville Bonanza*—what a silly name for a Texas yearbook—and searched for the photos of herself with her best friend, Nancy. They'd been inseparable since first grade, had stayed friends until Nancy's death in 1982. She thought about her nephew. Poor Jake. He'd been all alone then, out there on the Dead Horse with old R.J. depending on him. Martha wanted to take the teenager home with her, but R.J. wouldn't hear of it. Nancy had been his housekeeper for years; together they'd raised Jake.

The following year R.J.'s son and daughter-in-law had been killed in a car wreck, their son Bobby left an orphan. And Jake had been there for the old man, helping to raise a wild kid as best as he knew how.

Until, of course, he'd gotten married and moved

onto his own place. At least R.J. had done the right thing by leaving Jake that ranch. A man needed something of his own, her Ian always said whenever Gert made noises about them moving out to the Lazy K. Ian enjoyed his store, liked selling hardware and all that kind of thing. Martha had kept the books and they'd done real well, especially after Kate was older and Martha had taken that job at the town hall. She'd always been glad she'd lived in town.

"Mom?"

Martha looked up to see Kate standing in the bedroom doorway. "Hi. I didn't hear you come in."

"I tried to be quiet, in case you were asleep."

"Oh, I stay up later now that I don't have to get up for work in the morning." She shut the yearbook and set it aside on the nightstand. She'd been sitting on the edge of her bed and had been so engrossed in the yearbook she hadn't even put on her nightgown yet. "I guess your grandmother stopped writing?"

"Yes." Kate smiled and sat down on the bed beside her. "She let me straighten the piles. And I even swept the kitchen floor before she sent me home. I left the computer with her, though, so she knows I'll be back tomorrow." She reached over for the *Bonanza*. "Is this your class?"

"Yes." She waited while Kate thumbed through the book and found her picture.

"You were so pretty. You don't look like Gran, though."

"My father said I was the image of his mother." She gently took the book out of Kate's hands and held it on her lap. "Enough of all that," she said. "You've been digging around this stuff all day. What are your plans for tomorrow?"

"Emily and I were going to try to have lunch together if she could get a sitter. I told Gran I'd be out in the afternoon to do some work on the book and then I thought we could all go to the Steak Barn for dinner."

"It's closed on Mondays."

"Oh. Well, we'll go on Tuesday night instead."

"This is supposed to be your vacation," Martha sighed. "I can't believe your grandmother is making you help her write a book just because she wants to be on television."

"I don't mind. It's fascinating, actually." Her beautiful daughter smiled her father's smile and Martha blinked back tears. She missed Ian so much. "It's giving me ideas for the show," Kate added.

"Speaking of the show, my goodness, Kate, every time I turn it on someone's always pulling someone else into bed."

Kate laughed. "That's what the viewers want to see. Romance."

"Romance," Martha repeated, thinking of her own situation. "Well, I guess we could all use a little more of that."

"Are we talking about Mr. Jackson?"

"No, we are not." She stood up and went over to her dresser to find a nightgown. "He's just a friend." For now, though he'd kissed her good-night tonight.

"Emily said he's quite the town bachelor."

"Emily's mother-in-law keeps inviting him over for dinner."

"Does he go?"

"I don't ask," she said, picking out a chaste lavender gown. "It's none of my business." But she knew anyway, of course. Carl had gone once, thinking he was going to a dinner party. Party of two was more like it, but Irene had always been a little sneaky like that. Like not giving anyone the correct recipe for her lemon bars that year they'd tried a Christmas cookie swap.

When she turned around, Kate had the yearbook again. The girl had a one-track mind, just like her grandmother.

"Your best friend married your brother? That must have been wonderful."

"It should have been, but Hank wasn't an ideal husband." There. She'd spoken the truth without saying anything. It was a skill she'd honed over the years. Even Ian, bless him, never suspected a thing.

"Why not?"

"He drank. Like his father, Mother's first husband. Handsome, charming, all Texas good ol' boy, but with a streak..."

"A streak of what?" Kate prompted, an absolutely fascinated look on her face. For heaven's sake.

"A dark side," Martha said. "Like those people on your soap opera. Nice on one side, yet not so nice on the other. I guess alcohol can do that to a person."

"I guess. So Nancy married your charming, handsome alcoholic older brother. And then what?"

"Older *half* brother." Martha made a move toward the door. The bathroom was just across the hall and as good a place as any to hide from her daughter's questions. "They didn't live happily ever after," she said.

"What happened?"

"The usual things that happen when a husband spends more time in bars than at home. Kate, I'd like to get dressed for bed now."

"Oh." But she held on to the yearbook. "Do you mind if I look through this?"

"Of course not, but it smells," she pointed out. "You should air it out for a few days."

"I'll take it to show Emily tomorrow. It might take her mind off being ten months' pregnant." She kissed her mother good-night before leaving the room. "See you in the morning."

"Good night, Kate," Martha said, wishing Gert had never started this book-writing business. What was past should stay in the past.

And some secrets should stay buried. For everyone's sake.

"WE SHOULD BE LOOKING at our own yearbooks if we really want to laugh," Emily said. She lay stretched out on her living room couch while Kate served her tea and graham crackers. She set the 1955 yearbook on the table and reached for the crackers. "This is the only thing I can eat lately," she confessed, hiding the box under the couch. "If the kids find them, they'll be finished in five minutes."

"I think I can wait a few more years before looking at our pictures in the yearbook," Kate said, moving her chair closer. "I didn't really keep in touch with anyone but you and George. Are you sure you're feeling okay?"

"I'm fine. I'm sorry about lunch, though. I was looking forward to—Elly, honey, don't put that in your mouth."

Kate reached over and pried a sandal from the three-year-old's chubby fingers. "Elly, come sit with Auntie Kate?" She lifted the little girl onto her lap and gave her a hug before replacing the sandal on her fat bare foot.

"Mommy's gonna have a baby," the girl stated.

"Yes, she sure is." Kate thought Emily looked awfully pale and uncomfortable. "What can I do to help you, Em?"

"Pull the baby out with your bare hands."

"Why don't I take the kids out to the ranch for a while instead?"

"Masochist," Emily muttered, but she looked relieved. "You mean I could have a nap?"

"Sure. What are single friends for?"

"What about Gert? She might not want three little kids around." Emily struggled to a sitting position.

"Four kids, counting Dustin's son."

"How old is he?"

"Eight or nine, I guess. Maybe he and John could play trucks or something. I think there's a mud puddle behind the barn."

"If I have this baby while you're gone, you'll have to keep the kids for three days," Emily warned. "My mother-in-law may decide she could use a break, too."

"Martha will know where to find her. Stay

where you are," Kate said. "The kids and I will be fine."

"They have to wear seat belts in the car, and Elly has to sit in a booster seat."

"No problem," she promised, scooping the toddler into her arms as she stood. "They'll have a ball and I'll bring 'em home dirty so you don't feel too guilty about my baby-sitting."

"Guilty?" Emily chuckled, then winced as she tried to get comfortable. "Not a chance. Once in a while you career gals need a dose of how the other half lives."

The next adult she saw turned out to be Dustin, who came around the ranch house as she stepped out of the car. Danny was next to him, a small shadow of his father whose mouth fell open when he saw a carload of children.

"You kidnapped the Bennett kids," Dustin said. "*Now* what are you going to do with them?"

Kate unbuckled Elly's car seat and lifted her out of the car. "I'm going to show them horses and cows and anything else you have around here. Emily needed a nap."

He looked a little stunned as Jennie and John tumbled out of the car and grinned at Danny.

"Hi," John said, his face split into a wide grin. He was an outgoing child, like his father. "I know you."

"Danny," he said, leaving his father's side as

John reached back into the car and retrieved a couple of Tonka bulldozers.

"I told John that you liked trucks," Kate said, hoping Danny would take over and show off his play area.

"Yep." But Danny didn't budge. Kate exchanged an amused look with Dustin, who looked almost as surprised as his son that they had company.

"Come on, boys," Dustin said. "I'll show you the ranch."

"What about us?" Jennie took her little sister's hand. "Can we see, too?"

"Sure," the cowboy said, moving closer. "We can all go together."

Well, this was different, Kate mused. He was actually being nice. She didn't know why she was surprised, since he had been kind when she'd been in love with him. Kind, gentle and very, very sexy.

Kate sighed and wondered if she should start dating that lighting technician the show had just hired. Maybe she needed to get out more, spend less time working. The problem was obvious, though. She'd never seen anyone like Dustin Jones in New York.

He knew the ranch inside and out—knew enough to understand where and how to make changes, and what to put on hold. He'd taken a couple of the older outbuildings down, he told her, before they blew down in the next bad storm and caused injury to people or animals. He was painting the barn because Gert said a well-kept barn made a ranch look prosperous. The Bennett children had visited ranches before, of course, but horses and cows were a pretty good show no matter how many times they'd been seen before.

"This is so cool," John said, when they reached Danny's digging hole. He eyed the large area of dirt tracks and drying mud. "What are you making?"

"A lake. And a river. And a fort."

"I brought my dozers," the younger boy said, dropping them in the dirt. "Can I play?"

"Yeah." Danny smiled, still shy but recognizing a kindred spirit. "Sure." He looked over at Dustin. "We'll stay here."

"Nowhere else, right?"

The boy nodded, and Dustin turned to John. "It's very important, John, when you're on a ranch, to stay where you say you're going to stay." He pointed to the bunkhouse. "That's where Danny and I live, so you boys can go in there if you want." And then he turned and showed John the main house. "Mrs. Knepper—Kate's grandmother—lives there and there's a path to her kitchen door."

"That's where I'll be," Kate interjected, "with your sisters."

"I know her," Jennie said. "She's the oldest lady in town."

"That's right."

"Nowhere else," Dustin said. "The barn and the outbuildings and the corrals are off-limits unless I'm there with you." He smiled down at the younger boy. "Your mom would be real mad at me if anything happened to you and I don't want her yellin' at me, okay?"

John laughed. "Okay."

Dustin turned back to the girls. "Do you want to see the new calves?"

And that was that, Kate realized. The boys stayed in their construction zone while Dustin led the girls past several small barns toward a fence line that held his new stock. He showed them the calves and let them name the newest one. There was a breeze, though it was getting near the hottest part of the day.

"I'd better get the girls inside to see Gran. She'll be wondering where I am."

"I think she saw you," he said. "She doesn't miss much."

"We'll go get lemonade and birthday cake," Kate told the girls. But she looked up at Dustin. "Are you going to join us?"

"I have work to do." But he held her gaze and for one odd and crazy moment she thought he was going to bend down and kiss her. She knew he wanted to and she wondered if she would protest if and when he did it.

Of course not. She felt the familiar flutters in the pit of her stomach when he looked at her like that, as if he wished they were alone and horizontal. She'd seen that look before. And when she took the girls' hands in hers and walked them to see Gran, she wondered if she'd had a similar yearning expression on her own face.

DUSTIN CHECKED ON the boys, then went into the barn to work on the tractor. He'd told Gert he was sure he could get it started again. He was pretty damn good at fixing machinery, knew grasslands from years of studying and reading, and could train a horse to do just about anything a man required it to do. But when it came to women—when it came to *this* woman—he was so damn frustrated that he might as well make it easy on himself and just ride off into the sunset…alone.

Kate McIntosh was driving him crazy and she'd only been around for, what? A couple of days? Danny talked about how pretty and nice she was, Gert rattled on with "Kate said" this and "Kate did" that. The woman was about as useless as teats on a bull, with her fancy little computer and designer clothes and big eyes looking around the ranch as if she would know how to do it better.

He'd better remember that she'd left him. She'd

never explained, never said goodbye. And he'd gotten stubborn. And proud. Too proud to go to her and tell her he loved her, that he cared more than he'd said. And after her dad died, she'd left for college and never looked back, not at Beauville and not at the man who wasn't good enough for her.

He'd never been good enough for her, which rankled. He was a hell of a lot better a man than she'd given him a chance to be. Oh, he'd heard about her fancy career in New York. Read the article in the newspaper a couple of years back that even had a picture of her and one of the characters on the show, a toothy actor with a big head of blond hair who was supposed to be a big star.

Dustin made a concerted effort to keep his mind on the tractor engine and off Kate. It bothered him that he still cared, still felt like an awkward kid when she was around.

But if she ever looked at him like that again, he was going to kiss her. *Really* kiss her.

And damn the consequences.

"SURE IS NICE HAVING children around," Gert declared, leaning back in her chair. "I like the noise." She watched Elly to make sure she didn't fall off the kitchen chair, but she needn't have worried. The little girl knew how to kneel on a chair and lean over a table to eat birthday cake. Being the youngest in the Bennett family must have taught her a great deal early on. Jennie was lady-like and kept a watchful eye on her younger sister while trying not to stare at Kate, who must look pretty darn glamorous to a five-year-old. Martha had been serious like that, too.

"I hope Emily gets some rest," Kate said, looking for all the world like an anxious mother.

"Do you plan to have kids?" Gert knew it wasn't politically correct to ask young women that question, but she thought she could ask her grand-daughter just about anything. But then Dustin Jones came to mind and she thought, well, just about anything.

"Of course."

"Well, what are you waiting for?"

"The right man." She licked frosting off her fingers and moved the knife off the table.

"I'm glad you're not one of those women who goes to, you know," she said, lowering her voice, "one of those banks."

Kate grinned. "I'd rather have a baby the old-fashioned way."

"My mom's having a baby," Jennie said. "Any day now, she said, and she hopes it's a boy so we'll be even. You know, two boys and two girls." She looked at Kate. "You think my mom's okay?"

"How about if I call her in a little while and check?" Kate refilled the girl's glass with milk.

"I'd call her now but she said she wanted to take a nap."

"Oh."

"I don't like naps," Elly declared, frowning at Gert across the table. "Just babies do."

Gert nodded. "I hope you'll bring your new baby sister or brother out here to visit me." She looked at Kate. "It's not like you're going to bring me any babies to hold in the near future. What kind of man are you looking for, anyway?"

Kate shrugged, looking for all the world like one of those television stars she wrote stories for. Such a beautiful girl, who would have beautiful babies. "The right one."

"You're not going to find him in New York City," Gert grumbled. "There're plenty of fine men right here in town. Right here on this ranch, actually. There's one walking around out there— probably swearing over that old John Deere— who'd make a fine husband and a fine father."

"I wonder who that could be." Kate winked at Jennie, who giggled.

"This place needs kids, needs a family," Gert sighed, knowing full well Kate wasn't going to pay any attention to her advice.

"I'm going to take the kids home in a while, then I'll come back to work on the book. Mom's going to come back with me and we'll bring dinner. Is there anything special you'd like?"

I'd like to give you the ranch. I'd like you to come home and take over, with your husband—a nice Texas boy. I'd like to watch a baby or two come into this world and call the Lazy K home.

"There's still pizza left over from Saturday," Gert said instead, reaching over to help Elly wipe her face with a "Happy Birthday" napkin. "We could have that. Or you could make one of your meat loaves."

"Meat loaf it is," Kate said.

"And we'll invite Dustin and Danny," Gert said.

Heck, no one had ever called her a quitter.

CHAPTER ELEVEN

"YOU'RE NOT WATCHING the show today?"

"We're taped three weeks ahead during the summer, Gran." The all-too-brief summer break would end with frenzied attempts to complete story lines for the November sweeps, the all-important ratings war. And as soon as she returned, the meetings would begin and the next nine months of the show would be determined. The sponsor wanted something "different and trendy," while the viewers resisted the new paranormal story line and wrote asking for more romance. Kate found herself wishing she spent more time on her own life instead of the lives of the fictional characters of *Loves of Our Lives.* It simply wasn't as much fun as it used to be, when she was young and enthusiastic and more than willing to work eighteen hours a day. There had to be something more in her life, she knew, but what? And where?

Kate looked out the window and saw Danny and John heading their way. "Here come the boys.

They're going to want their share of cake and milk, or maybe sandwiches.''

"Such good children. We'll give them all lunch before you take them home,'' Gran said, looking as content as could be in her easy chair, a stack of old newspaper clippings on her lap. The girls sat nearby on the couch, a pile of Kate's childhood books stacked in between them. Elly was almost horizontal, her eyelids half-closed as her sister pretended to read a story aloud. "I should call Elizabeth, too, and see how she's holding up.''

"I can't believe she hasn't had that baby yet and made you a great-grandmother.'' Kate scribbled the ingredients for meat loaf on a piece of scrap paper. She could bake potatoes and pick up a fruit salad from the deli section of the supermarket. Gran would want green beans. "Maybe we should ask them for dinner, too.''

"Call them,'' Gert said. "See what's going on out there. We can have ourselves a little party.''

"Sure.'' It was better than Dustin as the only adult male at the dinner table. She really should grow up, Kate mused. She should get over her hopeless attraction to denim-clad men in cowboy boots. She should get over the undeniable sexual pull she felt every time she was within ten feet of Dustin Jones.

"Honey, do you see yourself living here someday?''

"Maybe," Kate said, looking out the window again. "After I've saved enough money."

"Having extra money is a good thing, don't get me wrong, but it won't buy happiness, never will," she declared. "This is a good place to raise children. Edwin and I did just fine. We didn't have much, but we managed."

"Your family was rich." She'd heard her grandmother's stories of growing up in the middle of a proud and prosperous ranching family, one of the oldest in the county if not the state, but Gert had been quiet about her first marriage. "What happened?"

"I was disinherited after I eloped with Hal," she said. "It was quite a scandal at the time. And my father wasn't the easiest man to get along with. He never got over my marrying that man, but my mother helped me out from time to time without my father knowing. Even after Hal died of influenza one winter, my father wouldn't let me in the house."

"That's terrible, Gran. What did you do?"

The woman smiled. "Oh, you'll know soon enough, when I get to that chapter."

"By the way," Kate said. "I thought I'd teach you how to use the computer. Don't frown at me like that. You can learn how to turn it on and turn it off and open your own file."

"I'd rather talk while you type. It's faster that

way and, after all, I'm ninety years old and not getting any younger." She set the clippings aside and struggled to her feet. "I'll help you with lunch, and then later we'll go back to storytelling. Katie Couric isn't getting any younger either."

"Okay." She turned back to the window. Dustin had joined the boys and had stopped walking to listen to something John had to say. Danny still had that shy grin on his face, an expression that tugged at her heart. The boy was too quiet, though, with secrets behind that shy smile and those dark eyes. "I found out Danny hasn't always lived with his father."

"No. I think Dustin is real new to fatherhood, but he does it well." She stood beside Kate at the window and looked out. "He's a fine-looking man," she said. "A girl could do worse."

"If a girl was looking," Kate amended.

"You're looking," her grandmother declared. "At *him*."

Yes, she was. And looking was safe enough.

Safer than touching. Or standing too close. Or, heaven forbid, kissing. She might as well be eighteen again, because she felt as awkward and curious as she had nine years ago. "You'd better start watching what you say. He's heading here with the boys."

"Good," her grandmother said. "We'll ask

them for supper and you can show him what a good cook you are.''

''I'm not auditioning for him, Gran.''

''It's a start.'' The old woman ignored her. ''Make a fresh pot of coffee, Kate. And let's see what the man wants.''

THE MAN WANTED KATE, of course. Simple biology, Gert figured. Mix the two of them together often enough and something would happen—such as Kate staying in Texas, and Dustin taking over the ranch permanently. Kate would be a good mother to that little boy. Heaven only knew where that ''Lisa'' woman was. Gert had asked a few questions, put two and two together. A few years ago a Lisa Jones had rented a garage apartment from the cousin of one of the ladies from church. She'd owed some rent, and the cousin had once commented that Lisa was ''bad news all around.''

Well, it didn't take a college graduate to understand that little Danny hadn't lived the kind of life anyone would want for a child. Somehow he'd ended up with Dustin, which certainly was the right place for the boy. Just like the ranch was the right place for Kate. She shouldn't waste her life on those slick city men, with their expensive suits and cologne. Gert even heard that men in the city got manicures, just like women. She'd never heard anything quite so silly in all her life.

She and Kate fed the little boys—to her disappointment Dustin hadn't joined them—and now Kate was off to town again, the Bennett children and Danny tucked into her car. Dustin would come for supper—Gert would see to it he couldn't refuse—and all Gert would have to do was prevent Martha and her opinions from ruining a budding romance. Jake and Elizabeth could be the perfect example of happiness. Gert knew her granddaughter; she wanted children and she loved the ranch. All Kate needed was a little push in the right direction.

"DON'T PUSH," JAKE hollered. "Pant."

Elizabeth glared at him. "I'm having minor—I repeat, *minor*—contractions, Jake. I am not pushing or panting or getting ready to deliver this baby on your grandmother's kitchen table, so please sit down and eat your meat loaf. It could be a while before you get another home-cooked meal this good."

"Thank goodness you're not in pain," Martha said. "Should we be timing them?"

"Not yet," Elizabeth said, picking up her fork and looking for all the world as if she intended to finish her supper. "I'm sure my husband will tell me when I'm ready." She laughed. She was about to have a baby and she was laughing. Kate was impressed.

"Can I get you anything?" Kate lifted the iced tea pitcher. "Something cold to drink?"

"We have beer," Gert added. "If you feel the need."

Elizabeth smiled. "I think I'll stick with the tea. Please don't look so worried. This could be false labor, you know. I've heard it happens."

"Whatever it is," Jake said, looking very pale, "we're going to the hospital to check it out."

"After dessert," his wife said. "And only if we need to."

Dustin and Jake exchanged worried looks, and Kate didn't feel so confident either. The remark about delivering the baby on Gran's kitchen table suddenly wasn't so funny. Elizabeth had a mind of her own, but there was no sense taking any risks.

"Dessert coming right up," Kate announced, standing to clear the table. Dustin rose to help, even though there was still food on his plate. Martha's eyebrows rose as the cowboy lifted her empty plate from in front of her.

"Excuse me," he said, then looked across the table at Kate and gave her one of his quick, rare smiles.

"Why, thank you," Martha said, flustered. "I can help, too."

"Stay there, Mom," Kate told her. "The coffee's ready and I'll serve the last of the birthday cake."

"There's still cake?" Gert frowned. "You'd think we'd have eaten it all by now."

"This is the last night," Kate promised. "Tomorrow we'll have apple pie at the Steak Barn."

"I love cake," Danny said. "'Specially this kind."

"You can have my piece, too," Gert told him. "I think I'm just about caked out."

"Ooh," Elizabeth inhaled, as her worried husband leaned closer.

"Another one?" She nodded, and Jake grew even more pale. He looked over to Dustin, who returned to the table with coffee mugs.

"We'd better go," was all he said, and Dustin nodded, banging the mugs on the table as he set them down.

"I'll drive you," he told Jake.

"Danny can stay here with me," Gert piped up, which made the little boy smile again.

"Take my car," Kate said. "She might be more comfortable in the Lincoln than in a truck."

Elizabeth allowed herself to be helped to her feet as soon as the contraction was over. "I'm sorry to miss dessert," she said, "but I wouldn't mind having this baby finally arrive. Kate? Come with us?"

"What?" Her first panicked thought was how on earth was she going to deliver a baby in the back seat of the Lincoln? She set the dessert plates on the table before she dropped them on the floor. "Are you sure?"

"I think I could use some female companionship right now." In other words, she didn't want to be alone with two frowning ranchers.

"Sure," Kate said, wiping her shaking hands on the sides of her shorts. "Should I bring anything?" Towels, she thought quickly. Boiling water. Rubber gloves. Bandages?

"Fill a thermos," Dustin said.

"With what?"

"Coffee. For the waiting room."

"I'll do that," Martha offered. Since no ranch kitchen held less than five thermoses, Martha easily prepared coffee while Kate ran to the bathroom and grabbed an armload of clean towels, just in case. Jake carried a protesting Elizabeth to the car and tucked her into the back set, then sat beside her and took her hand. Kate and Dustin hurried into the front seat and, once Martha had tossed the thermos into her daughter's lap, Dustin started the Lincoln and sped toward town.

"Should we call the doctor?" Kate moved the stack of towels aside and lifted her cell phone from her purse.

"Good idea," Jake said, but it was Elizabeth who told her the number she'd memorized. Kate dialed and left a message with the answering service.

"Three minutes apart," Elizabeth said anxiously. "Maybe this is going to happen faster than I thought."

Jake swore, and Dustin's fingers tightened on the steering wheel as the car went even faster along the straight empty road. Kate clutched the thermos and wished she'd taken CPR classes.

"I've seen it on your show," Elizabeth said in a breathless voice to Kate. "Babies are born in strange places all the time, right, Kate?"

"All the time," she agreed, thinking her cousin's wife had lost her mind. That was television. Carefully scripted, rehearsed scenes with plastic dolls for babies or, occasionally, a nice healthy infant for the close-ups. She glanced over at Dustin, who looked at her as if she really had lost all sense. "But contractions three minutes apart still gives us time to get you to the hospital." She hoped she sounded as if she knew what she was talking about. "I'll check with Emily," she said, punching the number into the cell phone. "Hi, George? It's Kate and—what?" She listened for a moment, then said, "Okay, good luck," before turning the phone off.

"What?" asked Elizabeth.

"Emily's in labor, too," she said. "George said she was taking a shower."

"A shower?" Jake repeated, incredulous.

"This is her fourth time," Elizabeth exclaimed, still sounding calm. "She's a pro."

"I guess we'll see everyone at the hospital," Kate said, turning around to see how Elizabeth was doing. She lay in Jake's arms, her legs stretched out on the seat, and looked for all the world as if she was enjoying herself. Jake, on the other hand, was a picture of a man about to fall apart. Grim and nervous, he clenched his jaw.

"Is this as fast as this thing can go?" he asked, frowning at the back of Dustin's head.

"Yeah," Dustin answered. "Without flying into a ditch."

"I don't want to give birth to my first child in a ditch," Elizabeth said. "Calm down, Jake. We're going to get through this."

"First and last child," he muttered.

"Uh-oh."

"What?"

"I think my water broke."

Kate tossed a couple of towels to Jake, who helped his wife spread them underneath her.

Dustin slowed down as they drove through Beauville and then sped up again as they flew past the former drive-in north to Marysville. "It won't be long now," he promised.

"Thank goodness," Elizabeth said.

"It's getting worse?"

"No, I don't think the contractions are coming

any faster," Elizabeth said. "But Jake's about to pass out."

"I am not," he said, but Kate wondered. She wasn't feeling so good herself. She looked at her watch at least twenty times on the drive to Marysville, though she was certain Dustin drove it in record time. He pulled up in front of the hospital's emergency room doors and before Dustin could open his door, two paramedics appeared to help Elizabeth from the car.

"Go park," one of them told Dustin. "We'll take it from here."

"Thank God," she heard him mutter under his breath as he put the car in "drive" and headed toward the visitors' parking lot.

"You did a great job getting us here," she told him, once he'd found a spot and parked. Once the engine was turned off it became very quiet and Kate was aware that the last time they had been in a car together they had taken off most of their clothes and made love.

"I haven't driven that fast since I was seventeen," he said, leaning back against the seat. He closed his eyes. "I was sure hoping she wouldn't have that baby in the car."

"That only happens on television," she assured him.

"Well, you would know." He didn't open his eyes as she leaned over and turned the key in the ignition, then pushed the button to lower her window. Almost sundown, the air had cooled slightly, just enough to be comfortable for a few moments.

"Is that supposed to be a slur on my job?" She turned the key to the off position, but before she could lean back Dustin took hold of her wrist to stop her.

"No," he said, looking down at her while he held her arm with gentle, calloused fingers. "I'm sure you got what you wanted."

"You make that sound like a bad thing."

He shook his head. "Nah." He released her, but Kate didn't move far. Instead she waited for him to explain. He just looked at the hospital and said, "I've never seen Jake so nervous."

"Weren't you nervous when your son was born?"

He turned to her and frowned, and she knew she'd somehow trespassed on forbidden territory. "What?"

She tried to sound casual, but she hoped that he would explain about Lisa and Danny and that summer. "When Danny was born. You and, uh, Lisa must have been pretty nervous yourselves."

He stared down at her.

"Danny," he repeated, as if he couldn't understand her. "You're talking about *Danny*?"

"It was a shock," she admitted, willing to get this out in the open. "I admit it. And I was glad to get out of town, especially after my father died.'' Dustin didn't say anything. "I saw you at the funeral," Kate said, remembering a time in her life that she'd rather not think about for too long.

He still didn't say anything.

"I guess I shouldn't have brought this up," she said, deciding she'd rather be delivering a baby than having this conversation. She shouldn't still care if he'd had sex with another woman and made her feel like the biggest fool in the world.

But Dustin surprised her. "We used to spend a lot of time sitting in my old Buick."

"Maybe we should go in," she said, thinking that sitting in a car—any car—with him again was certainly having a sensual effect that was extremely disconcerting. She thought she'd be over that by now, a mature woman of twenty-seven with a career, pension plan, matching furniture and a fistful of mutual funds.

"Not yet," he said.

He'd always had the most beautiful mouth. Kate gulped as he reached over and lifted her chin with his index finger. A familiar gesture, and her reaction was to lean closer as his mouth descended. It was the briefest brushing of lips, a mere whisper of what their kisses used to be. Then he kissed her again for a longer time, a kiss that promised hours of kissing and touching and lots, lots more. Kate wanted to sink into his arms, but she kept herself from reaching up to him, kept from moving any closer toward this man who could have her stripped naked in ninety seconds, tops.

Some things didn't change.

DUSTIN DIDN'T STOP her from leaving the car. He followed slowly, moving across the parking lot at his own pace.

So all along she thought Lisa Gallagher had had his baby. She'd left town because she thought he'd slept with Lisa and gotten her pregnant. And all along he had been sure—deep in his heart where it hurt the most—that Kate had left him because she'd finally realized the kid from the wrong side of town wasn't good enough for her.

CHAPTER TWELVE

"THIS ISN'T GOING to work, Mother." Martha rinsed the last of the dinner plates and stacked it in the drainer with the rest of the drying dishes. She'd dry them a little later, while the pans that held the meat loaves soaked.

"What isn't?" Gert looked up from the papers she'd spread all over the kitchen table. Once again, her mother was involved in this silly book business. You'd think a ninety-year-old lady would be content to crochet afghans, not spend her time airing the town's dirty laundry.

"Your matchmaking." She looked into the living room to make sure the boy couldn't hear. He was engrossed in a television show, having explained to "Grandma Gert" earlier that he and his Dad didn't have a television set in the bunkhouse and he sure missed "watchin' all the shows." He seemed like a nice enough child, though a little too quiet. But a quiet child was a refreshing change from some of the little hooligans Martha saw with their mothers in town.

"What are you talking about, Martha? I'm just a nice old lady happy to have the young folks around."

"Don't give me that," her daughter said, tossing the dish towel onto the counter. She sat down at the table and looked at her watch. "You're pushing Kate and that cowboy together, and don't you think I don't know it."

"She could use a man in her life."

Who couldn't? Martha wanted to reply, but she didn't discuss such things with her mother, never had. "Not that man," she said, lowering her voice to a whisper. She didn't want that little boy to hear. "I had to chase him off when they were teenagers. Those Jones boys were never any good."

"Dustin is a good man. And, Martha, you sound like an old witch."

Now that hurt. She didn't want to be called old, witch or not. "I just want the best for Kate."

"In New York?" Gert snorted. "She belongs here, and don't you tell me you don't miss her."

"Oh, I miss her, all right," she admitted. "And I'd do just about anything to see her married and happy and living close to me here in Texas, but everyone has to live their own lives, Mother. We just have to accept that Kate's life is in New York, working on that TV show."

"Speak for yourself, Martha," her mother said,

looking decidedly grumpy. "I don't have to accept any such thing."

Now would be a good time to change the subject, Martha decided. "I wonder how Elizabeth is doing. Poor Jake. He looked terrified that she would have that baby on the way to the hospital."

"I'm sure they made it," Gert declared. "First babies take their time."

"I remember." She'd been in labor with Kate for nineteen hours. Ian, her sweet, quiet, well-mannered Ian, had come close to assaulting the physician to make him do something. The pregnancy itself had seemed like a miracle after wanting a baby so many years. And then "labor" had been exactly that, before the days of so-called "natural" childbirth and all that breathing and panting the young women were so fond of. How proud her husband had been of that wrinkled red infant. "Maybe I should plan on sleeping here tonight."

"The boy, too," Gert agreed. "But Kate will call us, or Dustin will. We'll have news soon enough."

"I suppose," she said, turning around an old newspaper so she could read the headlines. "You're really enthused about this book, aren't you?"

"As the oldest living resident of Beauville, I

think it's important that I write my memoirs,'' she said.

"Nonsense," Martha replied. "You just like having Kate at your beck and call. And you like the idea of using her computer."

Gert chuckled and smacked the back of Martha's hand with a yellowed envelope. "You're a funny girl, Mattie," she said, using a pet name she hadn't used in years. Martha blinked back tears, silly tears she couldn't explain to herself. "You and Hank were as different as night and day that way."

"Hank had a mean streak." She avoided her mother's eyes and instead pretended to be interested in a yellowed copy of the Dallas paper.

"He must be dead," Gert declared, her voice devoid of emotion. "The last time I talked to him was March 5, 1965. He was falling down drunk and I told him to sober up before he killed someone."

"And what did he say to that?" Martha asked, though she'd heard the story before.

"He said some very unpleasant things," her mother replied. "He was worse than his father that way."

"What do you think happened to him?"

"In my book, I wrote that I think he died in a car accident somewhere. I pray to the good Lord that he didn't take anyone with him." She sighed. "Poor Jake."

"Poor Jake? He was spared, in my opinion. Nancy loved her job at the Dead Horse and R.J. was a better father than Hank could ever have been." Martha took a deep breath and waited for her mother to argue with that opinion, but Gert didn't seem to want to talk about her firstborn any longer.

"Here," she said, pushing the pile of newspaper clippings toward Martha. "Why don't you look through there and see if you can find anything about Beauville and World War I? My mother must have saved those for a reason."

"I suppose," she said, turning them around so she could read the headlines. Nineteen seventeen was safe enough; there was nothing in that year that could stir up trouble.

"IT'S GOING TO BE a while," Jake announced as he entered the hospital's second-floor waiting room. "Elizabeth wants me to send you two home."

"Yeah?" Dustin eyed his friend and former boss. Jake was looking a little gray around the edges. "We've only been here for half an hour." And ten minutes of that had been spent in Kate's car.

"Yeah," Jake said. "This could be a long night."

"We'll stay for a while longer," Dustin said,

wishing Kate wasn't standing so close to him. How in hell was he supposed to carry on a conversation when all he wanted to do was kiss her again? "I'll give Gert a call and fill her in."

"Wish Elizabeth good luck for us," Kate said, giving Jake a hug. "Can we get you anything? Coffee? Something cold?"

He shook his head and released her. "Thanks, hon, but we're all set. The nurses are taking good care of everything and Beth's real comfortable—except for the contractions. They're still three minutes apart, so the doctor said nothing is going to happen right away."

A lot had happened already, Dustin figured, remembering a very willing woman in the front seat of the Lincoln. Kissing her hadn't been in his plans—not even close—but she'd leaned over to turn the key and suddenly she was so close...and it was so easy to touch her, kiss her, taste her.

And so damn dangerous.

Dustin shoved his hands in his pockets and watched Jake hurry out of the waiting room and head back to his wife. They were alone in the small room; its walls were decorated with framed southwestern prints and worn blue-cushioned chairs sat at the edges of a blue-and-green rug.

"I'll call home," Kate said. "If you want to go home to Danny, just take the car. My mother can always pick me up later."

"The boy will be fine with Gert," Dustin said. "For a while longer, anyway." He watched her pull the cell phone out of her purse. "You can't use that in here," he said, pointing to a small sign by the door.

"I'll take it outside."

"I'll go with you." Dustin didn't question why he didn't want to let her out of his sight, but that's the way it was. He should be running from this woman he used to know, a city woman now with a life he could only imagine, and with men and love affairs of which he was immediately and irrationally jealous. He'd always hoped he'd see her again, but for some reason he'd pictured rescuing her—coming upon her while she stood on the side of the road with a flat tire or a broken fan belt, smoke pouring out from under the hood of her car.

And he would, of course, help her. She would be grateful. And he would, as the song played constantly on the radio this spring, ask, "How do you like me now?"

But he hadn't counted on being angry, either. Angry with her for believing the worst of him, for not even asking him if what she'd heard about Lisa was true.

And he was angry with himself, too, for having told her "no strings" and then fallen in love with her. Served him right, too, for being such a cocky bastard.

"Dustin?" He looked over to see her by the door of the room. She looked beautiful and uncertain and a little bit shy, as if she wasn't sure of him. Good. No reason why both of them shouldn't be uncomfortable.

"Coming," he said, wishing he could haul her out of this hospital and to the airport, where she would board a plane to New York and never return. He didn't need Kate McIntosh messing up his life now, not when he was trying to make a life for himself and the boy. He should be running like hell back to the ranch, back to his empty double bed with the cheap sheets and the faded blankets. Back to hard work and dreams of someday owning a piece of the Lazy K.

If he kept his mind on work, he would be fine. If he started remembering nights with Kate, he would get more than a little sidetracked.

He followed Kate down the hall, oblivious to the smell of medicine and the glances of the nurses. Instead he noticed that Kate still had the nicest little body he'd ever had the privilege of getting his hands on. She wore a simple T-shirt and a pair of black shorts, but he'd bet they cost more than a week's pay. She was the elegant type now, and maybe she always had been. When they stepped outside to the portico and she leaned against the wall, Dustin stood a respectable distance away. He watched her dial the phone, talk to Gert and then to her mother while he stood there, hands in his pockets to keep from touching her.

"Just a sec," Kate said, and held out the phone to him. "Gert wants to know if Danny can sleep at the house." He took it from her, brushing her fingers with his own.

"Gert? That would be fine," he told his boss. "Just let him fall asleep on the couch and I'll get him when I come home. Thanks." He handed the phone back to Kate, who spoke for another minute or so, trying to talk Martha out of coming to the hospital, and then tucked the phone away in her purse.

"My mother wants to be here," she said. "She's always been close to Jake."

"She's his aunt, right?"

"Yes, but her best friend is—was—his mother. I think she thinks his mother would want her to look out for him."

Dustin couldn't picture anyone worrying about Jake Johnson. The man was virtually unflappable, and those years on the Dead Horse with Bobby proved that Jake could deal with just about anything. Except childbirth, he thought, remembering the panicked expression in Jake's eyes when they'd arrived at the hospital. The man had looked as if he was going to drop to the pavement in a dead faint. "I worked at the Dead Horse when Elizabeth and her niece came to visit," he said. "I've never seen a man fall so hard so fast."

"So you met the niece from Paris?"

Dustin smiled. "Amy Lou. She caused quite a commotion at the ranch last summer. She and Bobby Calhoun were supposed to get married on the Fourth of July, but Amy went to cooking school in France and Elizabeth ended up marrying a cowboy instead."

"She and Jake are lucky." Kate moved to the door. "I guess we should go back in and see if there's any news."

"Lucky?" He shook his head and followed her, holding the door open so she could pass through. "Not lucky. Smart. They were smart enough to know what they wanted—marriage, family, a place of their own. And they got all three."

She hesitated. "And what about you? Didn't you have all that, too?"

"No," he said, heading toward the stairs. "But I have a boy to raise and, if I work hard and cattle prices don't drop, I'll have some money to invest in the Lazy K. Two out of three ain't bad."

SHE SPENT TIME jotting ideas in the small spiral notebook she kept in her purse. *Harry's baby would be stolen, and its mother would disappear. Christian would discover that he was sterile and he couldn't have fathered Harley's twins. A hos-*

pital scene where, while waiting for her mother to come out of a coma, Isabel would fall in love with a handsome stranger in the waiting room. He would turn out to be a serial killer, a mental patient or a Texas cowboy about to discover oil on his property. Or he was the reincarnation of the man Isabel used to be in love with and—

"Kate?" She looked up to see Dustin holding out a cup of coffee. "I thought we could use some," he said, handing her the cup.

"Where did you find more coffee?"

"The cafeteria was still open. I checked in with Jake, but he said there's still no baby. You look beat."

"Baby-sitting the Bennett kids will do that to a person." She moved the papers off her lap and opened the lid on the coffee. "I should check again and see if Emily's here, too."

"I'll ask this time," he said, and left the room as quietly as he'd entered it. Kate watched him, wondering if there was a woman in town who loved him. Wondering if Lisa, wherever she was, had deserved him. Surely she hadn't, though Kate didn't know why she was so sure of that. Her grandmother trusted him, Jake liked and respected him, his son worshipped him and she herself was, as she had been nine years before, attracted to him to the point of forgetting that she was the kind of

woman who usually had more sense than to make
love to a man in the back seat of a car.

She was also the kind of woman who sure
wouldn't mind doing it again.

CHAPTER THIRTEEN

"IT'S A GIRL," Jake announced. He entered the waiting room and accepted Kate's hug and Dustin's handshake and congratulations. "We're calling her Nancy, after my mother."

Kate blinked back tears. "That's so wonderful, Jake. My mother will be so thrilled."

"Her middle name is Comstock, Beth's middle name," he added, smiling broadly. "She weighs seven pounds, nine ounces and she's twenty-one inches long. Do either of you know what time it is in Paris?"

Dustin chuckled. "Seven or eight hours ahead of us, I think. Does this mean Amy Lou is going to return to Beauville?"

Kate hoped the niece would visit so she could meet her. Her mother alluded to Amy Lou as "the crazy niece who cooks." "She'll want to know she has a new cousin."

Jake nodded. "Beth is the only family the girl has, so she's been worried that something might happen. I'm supposed to call her because Elizabeth has gone to sleep.''

''She's all right?''

''Yeah. Just worn out.'' He looked at his watch. ''Not bad. We were only here for four hours. I passed George Bennett in the hall. It turns out Emily barely made it to the hospital also. I guess the poor guy thought he'd be delivering his baby himself.''

''Is she okay?''

''Yes, and George told me to tell you he'd be—'' He turned as Emily's husband stuck his head in.

''It's a girl,'' he said, beaming. ''Healthy and screaming her lungs out. Em's fine and says she'll see you tomorrow for lunch.''

''That's a joke, right?'' There was no way to know, not with Emily.

''Yep,'' her husband, a beefy ex-high school football player, said. ''Go home. You all look exhausted.''

''Congratulations,'' Dustin told him, walking over to shake his hand. ''Four kids. I don't know how you do it.''

''We're crazy, that's all,'' he said, still grinning. ''You know what it's like raising kids.''

''Yeah,'' Dustin said. ''They keep you busy.''

''Hey, Kate,'' George called, on his way out the

door. "Thanks again for taking the kids to the ranch today."

"Any time," she answered, wishing for a moment that she lived in town and could spend more than a few hours a year with her best friend. Jake turned to follow him.

"I'd better get back, just in case Beth wakes up and needs something. Do you want to see little Nancy?"

"How do we do that?"

"Follow me," Jake said, his voice ringing with pride. "She's in the nursery so Beth can sleep." Kate grabbed the empty thermos and her purse, then hurried to catch up with him as they headed down the hall. Sure enough, the baby Jake pointed to was being held by a nurse. "That's her."

"She's beautiful," Kate said, completely awed by the appearance of this new person into the family.

"Are you sure you don't want a ride home? You look like you could use some sleep," Dustin said.

"I'm fine. One of the nurses said there was a cot I could use, so I'll sleep later." He grinned. "I'm too excited to close my eyes. I'll see you two tomorrow. Thanks for everything."

Kate wrenched her gaze from the baby and turned to her cousin. He looked tired, but triumphant. "Should I call Mom and Gran or will you?"

"I'll call them right now," Jake promised, "if you think they're still awake."

"Mom will be. She's staying at the ranch tonight."

"Sure."

"And Jake? Congratulations," Kate said, tearing up. "That little girl is very lucky to have you for a father."

"A father," he repeated. "I'm going to be the kind of father I wish I'd had."

"Yeah," Dustin said. "I know what you mean."

"COME ON," DUSTIN SAID, tugging Kate away from the glass. Eight little babies, in various moods, lay in their bassinets or in a nurse's arms. And they seemed to have the oddest effect on Miss New York City standing beside him. She made smiley faces and waved and even talked baby talk when George lifted his new daughter to show her off. The newest Bennett was already plump and pink, with a strange shock of red hair sticking up from the top of her head. They'd caught another brief glimpse of little Nancy—a tiny round face peering out of a pink blanket—as she was taken into her mother's room.

"Just a minute," Kate said, pointing for George to come over to the door. "What's her name?"

she mouthed, before the nurse opened the door to let her speak.

George shrugged. "Emily's still thinking. She said she was too tired to make a decision."

"Oh. Well, tell her I'll stop in tomorrow and find out."

"Sure. Hey, make that cowboy take you home," he called before the nurse shut the nursery door.

"There," Dustin said, figuring he needed to take her arm and remove her physically from the building. "You've had your orders."

"Okay," she said, but with great reluctance.

"I didn't know you liked babies so much."

"Why wouldn't I like babies?"

He shrugged, figuring he should have kept his mouth shut, and headed for the stairs. "I don't know. You have the fancy career and all." He didn't feel like talking about babies and he sure didn't feel like waiting for an elevator to go down one floor. He wanted to get out into the fresh air and away from those excited fathers. Fatherhood was tough enough with an eight-year-old; he didn't know how Jake and George could be so excited about starting from scratch.

"What about you?" she asked, keeping up with him as they hurried down the stairs to the lobby.

"What about me?" He crossed the antiseptic-smelling area in quick strides and pushed the door open for Kate to go through first.

"Do you want more children?"

"Hell, no." He hadn't really wanted the one he had, but he couldn't say that. Danny was a decent boy, but it wasn't easy trying to build a home for him. And a future. Life had been a lot easier when he'd been alone, during the years he'd left Beauville and worked on other ranches. He'd returned to the Dead Horse a few years back and stayed away from his brother's troubles for as long as he could. And then he'd done what he had to do for the sake of the boy. Danny was family, after all. "I'm not figuring on getting married real soon."

"Does Danny see his mother at all?"

"Not if he's lucky." He was too tired to worry about what Kate thought, he realized. He'd been up since four, trying to get a lot of the heavier work done before the heat of the day. He didn't like to work the horses in this heat unless it was the crack of dawn.

"She's that bad?"

"Yeah," he said, knowing that Kate, with her perfect parents and perfect childhood would never be able to understand. "That bad." She had that look on her face as if she wanted to ask a lot of questions, so Dustin braced himself to withstand the onslaught.

"Want me to drive?" She held out her hand for the keys. "You look beat."

"I'm not that tired," he said. "We'll stop at the

truck stop and get breakfast before we head home. It's after two already and I just realized how hungry I am."

"We used to do that after the movies." And then she blushed, remembering, as he did, exactly how they had worked up an appetite.

"Yeah. There were a lot of things we used to do." He unlocked the doors, held the passenger door open for her and went around to the driver's side of the car. She still had a great set of legs. And a great rear end, too. And since he'd never been accused of being brilliant, here he was fantasizing about making love to this woman. Again.

He'd started up the car and was halfway out of the parking lot before she spoke again.

"Remember the time the sheriff almost caught us?" Kate asked, turning toward him with a wry smile on her face. "We hadn't known the movie was over and everyone else had left."

"He figured I was up to no good, all right."

"I talked him out of arresting you and not telling my dad."

"Your father would have come after me," Dustin said.

"No, he wouldn't," she said. "I think he liked you. It was my mother we would have had to worry about."

"She's still someone I don't want to tangle with," he admitted, and Kate smiled at him.

"I know what you mean. She's probably worried about us being together right now, in the middle of the night, without Jake and Elizabeth to chaperone."

"I have an idea," he said, stepping on the gas. "We'll get breakfast, if you can wait another twenty or thirty minutes."

"Sure, but why—"

"For old time's sake," he said. "And because I'm starving." And also because he didn't know when or how he would have the chance to be alone with her again. He didn't want to think about making love to her, but there was something about Kate that made him think of nothing else. Maybe it was time to get it out of his system once and for all. And from all indications, Kate would agree.

"WE'RE TRESPASSING," Kate whispered, holding the bag filled with fast-food breakfast items on her lap. The coffee, sitting in the cup holders, smelled delicious. She was suddenly ravenous, she realized as she peered out the window at the Good Night Villas construction site.

"You don't have to whisper," he said, guiding the car past the building toward the back of the property. "There's no one around."

That was true. She felt a little more at ease when Dustin found the spot off to the side in back, where the original parking area hadn't been disturbed, and shut off the car engine and lights. He switched the interior light on so Kate could distribute the food, but turned it off again when they had their breakfast sandwiches on their laps.

"This is very strange," Kate said, after she'd eaten half of an egg- and cheese-filled croissant.

"Why?"

"You and me. Here. With our clothes on."

"You can take your shirt off," he offered, "if it would make you feel better."

"No, thanks." She hoped he was only joking. "We'll just stay dressed and act like adults," Kate said, though the temptation to toss the uneaten food back into the bag and climb into the back seat was certainly unsettling. "What would you have done if it was me who had gotten pregnant that summer instead of Lisa?"

Dustin choked on his English muffin egg sandwich, so Kate handed him a napkin and waited for him to catch his breath. "For cripe's sake, Kate," was all he could say, "what made you bring that up?"

"We're sitting here at the scene of the crime, so to speak. It's nine years later, and I want to know."

"I would have married you, of course, if your parents didn't kill me first."

"Really?"

He frowned at her. "Well, of course. What kind of a question is that?"

She shrugged and took a sip of the coffee, which was pretty terrible stuff. "I've always wondered."

"Yeah? What else have you wondered?"

"Why you had sex with her at the same time you were having sex with me." There. She leaned back against the car door and watched him, wondering if he would give her the answer to the question that had bothered her for years. "I know that was a long time ago," she added, not wanting him to think this was something she dwelt upon on a regular basis. "But this seems a good time and place to ask."

"Yeah?" He set his coffee cup on the dashboard. "Nine years later seems like a good time to ask? Did you ever think of asking me any of this before you kicked me out of your life?"

She remembered that night all too well. She'd been hurt and embarrassed and miserable because she had fallen in love with him. He'd warned her beforehand. He'd said, "No strings, sweetheart." And she'd foolishly believed she could make love to him without her heart getting broken. "No. I was too angry."

"*You* were angry?" He stared at her, his gaze intense upon her face. She wanted to look away, but she didn't. "Look, Kate, you asked me a question. I answered it. I didn't grow up rich and pampered in a big house on Apple Street facing the park. I had a pretty crappy home life, Katie, but if you were the one who'd gotten pregnant that summer I would have married you and done whatever I could to make you happy. Does *that* answer your question?''

"I guess it does." She wished she could see Dustin's face, but the interior of the car was fairly dark except for the dim glow of the construction site spotlights coming in through the back window. She reached her hand out to touch his arm.

He tugged her toward him. "There's something about sitting in a car with you—"

"Do you think it's an automobile fetish?"

"Definitely," Dustin whispered. Their lips were almost touching, and then came the kind of kiss she remembered—and had tried to forget. Her arms looped around his neck and the half-eaten breakfast sandwich slid off Kate's lap and onto the seat. He tasted of coffee when her tongue touched his when her lips parted to allow him entrance. She moved closer, not noticing that her knee squished an uneaten square of fried potatoes or her coffee was perilously close to tipping out of the cup holder. All Kate knew was she was kissing Dustin again, at the Good Night Drive-In, and all was right with her world.

His hands held her waist, then inched up under her blouse to smooth her skin. Oh, yes, Kate thought, murmuring a little sound of approval as his fingers touched her. He was still the best kisser she'd ever known, with the most tantalizing long fingers and a way of moving his tongue that made her want to wrap her arms around his neck and hang on. And she did.

Kate didn't know if she was eighteen or twenty-seven, if it was sunrise or sunset, if she was in Manhattan or Beauville. None of that mattered anyway. His hand was on her breast and his tongue tangled with hers and everything was as it should be. Familiar and yet so amazing and different, kissing Dustin brought back memories of hot sex and even hotter Texas nights.

"Damn bucket seats," he muttered, after easing his mouth from hers.

"I should have rented a van."

They tried to catch their breath, but it wasn't easy. Kate could feel the heat emanating from his body and knew her own was equally warm, willing and able. Her brain and common sense disappeared when he lifted her and easily positioned himself in the passenger seat, with Kate on his lap.

Straddling him was a heavenly position, Kate decided. Not ladylike or remotely subtle, but an easy angle from which to lower her head and kiss him. She felt his arousal through layers of cotton and resisted wriggling against him. Kissing was enough for now, and his fingers fumbling with the buttons of her blouse more than enough stimulation to make brain activity impossible.

Leaning into his body would guarantee that she was lost, so Kate held herself back. But clearly Dustin had other ideas. Once her blouse opened, he moved his hands to her waist and tugged, bringing the heat of her against the hardness of him and setting them both on fire. Clearly, Kate thought in a haze, there would be no turning back. And, with the delicious sensations radiating from her body, why would she want to?

Dustin's hands moved to the waistband of her shorts and found her zipper as Kate attempted to unbutton his shirt. She used to be better at this, she remembered, but—

"You're trespassing," came a loud male voice, and a beam of light shone on Kate's face, making her open her eyes and then close them again before she went blind. Dustin released her, then turned toward the intruder. The windows were open, so the flashlight came closer. "This is the deputy sheriff. You two, break it up. You're under arrest."

"THEN WHAT HAPPENED?" Emily tucked her baby against her breast and rearranged the blankets so that nothing was exposed. She was due to leave the hospital this afternoon, but had convinced the nurses she needed a few more hours rest before going home to care for four children. "Was it Carter? He picks up all the extra hours he can since he got engaged. I think he's saving up for a house."

"Yes. And Dustin knew him. He went to school with Dustin's older brother."

Emily chuckled. "It's still a small town. Lucky for you."

"Not exactly. I guess Darrell, the brother, had—has—quite a reputation in the county. It took a while to convince the man that we weren't there to steal construction supplies or deal drugs. He finally caught on that we were two stupid adults making out in a rental car, but it took forever before he let us go."

"And then what?" Emily leaned forward, her eyes sparkling. "Tell me you had sex with him."

"I did not have sex with him." But she certainly would have, if the Beauville sheriff's deputy hadn't interrupted. "I'm not sure things would have gone that far."

"Hah," her friend said. "Your face gets red every time you talk about him."

"It's because of our past together."

"It's because you're on vacation and he's around and you're around and—" she waved her free hand to indicate the cheery hospital room— "one thing leads to another and then you're in here having your fourth baby."

"Speak for yourself," Kate said, but her gaze

was on the little girl who was intent on nursing. "She really is beautiful."

"Then have a few of your own," Emily said. "Grab that cowboy and take him back to the drive-in tonight. Or here's a novel idea—why don't you ask him out?"

"On a date?"

"Don't they do that in New York?"

"They do, but—"

"No 'buts,'" Emily insisted. "I want you to stay here in Beauville with me and Elizabeth and Lorna. Our kids can grow up together and raise hell while we complain and drink frozen margaritas and give birthday parties."

"I'd need a husband first."

Emily grinned. "Now why do I think that wouldn't be any trouble?"

"He was never in love with me," Kate said, knowing Emily would know who she was referring to. "So there's no reason to think he'd fall in love with me now."

"No?"

"No," Kate declared. This was the problem with being a romantic. She was a writer with a wild imagination, and he was a rancher trying to relive the good old days. These kinds of sexual journeys into the past never worked.

And she'd better keep reminding herself that if she got hurt again, she had only herself to blame.

CHAPTER FOURTEEN

SHE'D HOPED TO keep the drive-in incident quiet, but Kate realized she should have known that her mother would hear of it.

"I knew he'd get you in trouble," Martha declared, shaking her head outside of Emily's hospital room. It hadn't taken her mother long to track her down this morning. Martha was on her way out the door of the ranch when Kate finally woke up. It had been a long, sleepless night. "Those Jones boys are no good. He almost got you put in jail for trespassing!"

"It wasn't exactly—" Kate tried, moving her mother toward the nursery window so the sight of the babies might distract her.

"Carl thought it was somewhat humorous," her mother continued, having declined Kate's offer of a ride to Marysville this morning because the real estate mogul had offered first. "The sheriff's office called him at two this morning to check out your story. It's a good thing Carl knew who you are."

"I'm sorry they had to wake him," Kate said,

taking her mother's elbow and moving her toward the babies in the window. "Have you seen Elizabeth? Doesn't she look wonderful?"

"Yes, of course she does, but Kate, how on earth could you start up a relationship with that man?"

"It's not a relationship. It was just…" Kate hesitated. "I don't know what it was," she fibbed, knowing it was lust, pure and simple. On both sides. And it had felt great, before the deputy sheriff's intrusion.

"It's embarrassing, that's what it is," her mother informed her. "I know those kind of men, and they're no good."

"Mom, what on earth are you talking about? Dustin's a perfectly nice man, who happens to work for Gran. I've known him for years. Oh, look, here we are in front of the babies. Aren't they sweet?"

"You won't find little Nancy in there," Martha said, barely glancing toward the infants. "Your grandmother is still holding her in Elizabeth's room. Did you get pictures?"

"I sure did. Where's Carl? I'll apologize to him in person."

"He's visiting a friend of his father's who had surgery. I'm going to meet him at noon and we're going to have lunch on the way back to town. How is Emily?"

"Fine, of course. She's going home later."

"I'll stop in and say hello. Oh, is that the Bennett baby?" She pointed to the glass, where George was bundling up an infant to cradle in his arms. "Such a good father, that man," Martha said. "You should be so lucky to find a man like that, instead of fooling around with actors and cowboys."

"You know, Emily and George did their share of making out at the Good Night Drive-In, too," Kate pointed out. "Jennie may even have been conceived there, Mother."

"Oh, stop your teasing," Martha said, waving to George, who grinned at them and held up his new daughter.

"Teasing? I'm serious. And there's nothing wrong with cowboys," Kate replied, remembering Dustin's hands on her skin. Those very skillful hands had been heading toward her breasts when James Carter decided to earn his moonlighting money.

"Are we going out to dinner tonight?" Kate added.

"Oh. Yes." Her mother didn't look as excited as Kate thought she'd be about filet mignon and peach shortcake with freshly whipped cream tinged with cinnamon, a tradition when Kate was home on vacation. "I almost forgot that was tonight."

Her mother was more interested in what Carl

Jackson was doing tonight, Kate supposed. This behavior wasn't typical of her pleasant, overprotective, domestic and contented mother. For a split second Kate wondered if Carl had shown Martha his construction site one late night, but then she thought better of it. Martha McIntosh, age sixty-four, would never be caught dead in a compromising position.

For the thousandth time, Kate thought about kissing Dustin last night. Her mother was missing a lot of fun.

THERE WERE SOME things a man wanted to dwell upon and some things that didn't bear thinking about twice, Dustin decided. He'd spent the morning riding fence, checking water supplies and listening to Danny chatter on and on about Grandma Gert and Aunt Martha. Since when had the boy made Kate's cranky mother an honorary relative? No, he didn't want to think about the disapproving glances Kate's mother gave him whenever he walked into a room. And that he wished he could stop thinking about the way Kate felt in his arms last night, all trembling and warm and very, very willing.

Like the past nine years had never happened. Put the two of them together and it was just so damn hard to remember that they hadn't seen each other since they were teenagers.

Kate wasn't at the ranch now. He'd seen her take Gert in her car, most likely heading to the hospital to see that baby, and he'd seen Martha leave with Jackson, who was sure to tell about last night.

This would be a good day to lie low, Dustin figured. He'd work on remembering that he was a father now, with a ranch to run and money to make. He shouldn't be lusting after an ex-girlfriend as if he had no more sense than a longhorn bull.

"Daddy?" Danny's voice broke into his thoughts, and Dustin glanced toward the boy who was hanging on to the door of the pickup as if he was afraid of being tossed out the window.

"What?"

"Where's my mom?"

"I don't know," which was the honest truth, but Dustin didn't add "and I don't give a damn," which also was the truth.

"Am I gonna live here with you all the time?"

"Yeah," Dustin promised. "Remember how I told you we have to talk to the judge and make everything legal? Well, we're set to do that in a few weeks."

"Lee-gal," the boy repeated, liking the sound of the word. "Everything legal."

"Yeah. That's right." And Lisa would never be able to get her hands on the boy again. Lisa Gallagher Jones sure as hell didn't deserve any rights to her son.

"Are you gonna get a wife?"

Dustin chuckled and stopped the truck at a metal gate. He hopped out and pushed the gate open before returning to the truck. The boy was too small to open and close gates, but one of these days he'd be big enough to help out.

"Why do you think I need a wife?" he couldn't help asking as he drove through the gate and parked again.

The boy shrugged. "To make dinner and cake and stuff like that."

"We have Grandma Gert for that." God, it was hot today. He wiped his forehead and thought once again about Kate and last night. He'd have given a lot to take her home to bed, to have spent the night making love to a warm and willing woman who had the sweetest way of parting her lips—

"Daddy," Danny said. "What about the gate?"

"Yeah," he said, realizing he almost forgot to close the damn thing. He climbed out of the truck and pushed the heavy metal gate shut, making sure it was latched securely, before striding back to the Ford. If she was any other woman he'd take her out for dinner or into Marysville to see a movie, then for drinks and some snuggle-up dancing at the Last Chance. But she wasn't just any woman. Now she was Kate, big city lady, with fancy clothes and an even fancier attitude.

Dustin stopped short of the truck and looked at what he had to offer a woman like that: a dusty three-year-old truck, some shares in a struggling cattle venture, a bed in the bunkhouse and a little boy recovering from a broken heart. It wasn't much, he knew. And no amount of great sex would convince Kate McIntosh even to consider staying in Beauville past next week.

"WELL, THAT'S A REAL nice picture," Gert said, admiring herself on the front page of the "What's Happening" section of the *Beauville Times*. "That Danny's such a cute little fella."

Martha muttered something Gert couldn't hear, then raised her voice. "He looks as if he's one of the family, for heaven's sakes. And look, there's Kate standing there like she's his mother."

"I told you they were perfect for each other." Gert didn't mind needling her daughter now and then, just to hear her squawk.

"He's a nice enough child," Martha admitted, having spent Monday evening teaching him card games and feeding him cake. Gert had seen her make sure the boy was comfortably settled on the couch, with a light on so he wouldn't wake up in a strange place and be afraid.

"You need grandchildren," Gert declared.

"Shh," Martha warned, settling herself onto the couch. "She's coming down the stairs now."

"Kate?" Gert peered over her pile of scrapbooks to see if Kate had found the photo albums. Sure enough, her granddaughter had an armload of them. "I'm glad I thought of putting pictures in my book," she said.

"Yeah, I think the pictures will really—"

"Are we going over to see Jake's baby again tomorrow?" Gert interrupted. She liked babies, and she figured Kate's exposure to the little sweethearts might just keep her in Texas.

"Sure. They'll be home from the hospital." Kate set the photo albums on the floor at Gert's feet. "We'll bring them some casseroles."

"About this book," Martha began, frowning before she sneezed. "Who have you told about this, Mother?"

"Just the family. And that man friend of yours." Gert reached for the top album. What she wanted was a picture of herself with her horse. For the cover.

"Did you by any chance tell Doris Hansen?"

"The librarian? Why yes, when I did my research a few weeks ago. She seemed interested."

"Well, it's all over town that you're writing a book and several people came up to me at bridge this afternoon and asked me about it."

"What'd they want to know?" She was up to

the 1940s now and still going strong. Kate had only been home a few days and already she'd taught her grandmother how to run that mysterious computer. It wasn't so hard after all, Gert decided, as long as you didn't hit too many keys at once and didn't spill anything on it. Once you got the thing turned on it pretty much told you what to do, though she forgot how to turn it off and had to follow Kate's written directions each time.

"I'm not sure," Martha answered. "I think folks are a little suspicious of the whole thing."

Kate looked amused. "Do people in Beauville have that many secrets?"

"Well," Gran said, "Doris Hansen's great-grandfather was said to have escaped a murder charge in California by jumping on a train. When he woke up, he was in Beauville."

"Mother," Martha said, pushing the photo albums aside as if they were dead cats. "I don't know why you think you have to resurrect the past."

"We've had our share of problems, too," Gert declared. "Your brother—wherever he is—caused his share of heartache."

"Amen to that," Martha breathed.

"And his father wasn't much better," Gert added. "I've written that part already. Now I'm at the time when the boys were going off to war."

"It's very good so far," her writer granddaughter said. "Gran has a terrific memory for details."

"All I'm saying is that no one wants their dirty laundry aired in public, Kate. What's private should stay that way."

"Mom, I'm beginning to think you have a deep dark secret you don't want anyone to find out."

Gert raised her eyebrows at that. The guilty expression on Martha's face proved Katie right. "Is that so, Martha? And can I use it in the book?"

Her daughter stood up and picked up her purse. "I'm not going to listen to this kind of talk," she said. "Besides, I thought we were going out to dinner tonight."

"It's only three o'clock, Martha," Gert felt obliged to point out. "You want to eat at three o'clock?"

"I'm going to get my hair done," her daughter said. "I'm thinking of a blond rinse. And I'm tired of talking about secrets." With that, she swept out of the room. A few seconds later the back door slammed and, sure enough, when Gert leaned back in her chair and peered out the front window, she saw Martha's car making dust as she headed out to the highway.

"My goodness," Gert declared, chuckling at her granddaughter. "Your mother's a little edgy lately, don't you think?"

"Maybe she's spending too much time with Mr. Jackson."

"Or not enough," Gert pointed out. Seemed like Martha might need some male companionship. The woman had to get lonely; after all, Ian had been gone for nine years. "Your father was a fine man, but it just might be time for your mother to marry again."

"Marry? She's talking about moving into those retirement villas, not getting married." Kate didn't look too pleased.

"I'm sure you both miss your father," Gert said. "That heart attack took him so fast, I've never seen anything like it."

"I couldn't wait to leave and go to college," Kate admitted. "The house was so empty without him."

"Maybe Martha's feeling the same way now." She managed to lift herself out of the chair and wandered over to the kitchen window. "Dustin's back. His truck is parked by the horse barn. You haven't been riding yet, have you?"

"No."

"I still keep a few horses," Gert said. "They could use some exercise, if someone wanted to go out there and saddle them up."

"I'll ride tomorrow morning," she said, "when it's not too hot. I'm going to get the rest of my things from town and spend the rest of my vacation here. That way I can get some work done.''

''What kind of work?'' She watched for signs of the man or the boy. Sometimes Dustin stopped in to tell her what was going on. She liked that, when he'd come over and talk to her about cattle and feed and how the water was holding up. The boy would drink lemonade or milky, sugared coffee and it would be like the old days, when she ran this place and the foreman—Sandy, that was his name—would check in and see what she thought needed doing.

She liked a man who knew how to communicate. Gert turned toward her granddaughter, a young woman who didn't have the sense to know she had a place in the world and a good man to claim. Kate was pretty and smart, independent, too—a good thing in a woman, Gert knew, because it kept you from depending on other people to make you happy—but she should be running the Lazy K. She should be having babies and making love to a hardworking man who would work along with her and make something of their lives together.

''Kate,'' Gert said, and her granddaughter looked up from the photo albums, ''the barn needs painting real bad.''

''Dustin said he was working on it.''

''The man doesn't have time,'' Gert said, sighing to show how worked up she was about it.

"And I just get so depressed looking at that barn now and seeing how run-down it looks."

Kate untangled her legs and walked over to look out the window, too. "Well," she said, "I have ten more days. You must have a ladder around here somewhere."

"Dustin can do the high spots. If you could work on the barn and then maybe the outbuildings it would sure be a big help." And it would put Kate outside with the cowboy, who sure as shootin' wouldn't be able to stay away from her.

"Sure."

"We'll stop and get more paint and brushes tonight in town," she said. Painting could lead to other things, of course. Gert hid her smile of satisfaction and then decided to try one more thing. "Why don't you make a fresh pot of coffee? I could use a cup myself, and Dustin might stop by."

"Dustin? Why?"

"Well, to tell me how things are going," Gert explained. "He usually comes by around three-thirty." And he would come if she hung a red rag in the window. That was their private signal, one that meant Gert wanted to talk. She rummaged through her linen drawer—Kate must have rearranged it—while Kate fussed with the coffee grinding machine she liked so much. It only took a second to tuck the edge of the red bandanna into the window latch.

CHAPTER FIFTEEN

"YOU'RE GOING TO finish painting the barn," Dustin repeated, as if he'd never heard anything so crazy in his life. Kate set a mug of coffee in front of him and ignored that she was only inches away from him. If they were alone she'd sit on his lap and start kissing him again, so it was a good thing Gran and Danny were in the room. In fact, she noticed, the chaperones were destroying a perfectly good cup of coffee by adding large amounts of cream and sugar.

"Yes." Kate brought her own cup of coffee to the table and sat down across from Dustin. "It was Gran's idea. She's doing most of her own typing now." And she'd cleaned out the refrigerator, scrubbed the cupboards and washed the kitchen floor until the old linoleum turned a shade lighter. "And she'd like some of the outbuildings painted."

He frowned and turned to her grandmother, who was busy dishing out cookies to Danny.

"They're only store-bought," Gran explained,

plopping several chocolate chip cookies onto Danny's napkin. "But I like 'em anyway."

"Yeah," the boy said. "Me, too."

"Gert," Dustin said, trying to get her attention. "I'll get the barn done myself, but Kate—"

"Is perfectly capable of holding a paintbrush," Kate finished for him. "I've done it before."

"Not in this kind of heat you haven't."

"I'll wear a hat." She would show him. Maybe she wasn't baking cinnamon rolls or having babies or training horses, but she could dip a brush into a bucket of paint and slap it on the side of a barn.

"You'll start at dawn then," the man said. "You can't work much past nine, not in these temperatures."

"What time is dawn?" she asked, though she thought she should know, having been out with him until three-thirty or so the other morning.

"Five." Dustin took another sip of coffee. "I'll meet you on the west side of the horse barn tomorrow morning."

"You're going to paint, too?"

"No. I'll just get you started, get a ladder, things like that." That's when he looked at her and smiled. "I'll bet ten bucks you're not an early riser, are you?"

"I can manage," she promised. "Don't worry about me."

"Kate's a good worker," Gert declared, passing

Dustin a plate full of cookies. "'Course she doesn't belong in New York, but that's her business. She'd be better off comin' home and takin' over the Lazy K."

"Gran—"

Dustin turned that cool gaze her way again. "So why don't you?" He really was handsome, better looking than nine years ago.

"I—" she began, then stopped when she realized she didn't have an answer. Her home was here, in Texas, but her job—her career—was in New York. But was she really happy working seventy-hour weeks and dealing with the insanity of an hour-long television show that ran five days a week?

"See?" Gert chuckled. "My granddaughter is speechless. That doesn't happen very often."

"I'm a television writer. I don't know anything about running a ranch," Kate said, leaving the table on the pretense of getting the coffeepot. She would refill cups that didn't need refilling and try to change the subject back to painting barns. "We'll get more paint tonight when we're in town."

"I've got plenty," Dustin said. "Enough to get you started, anyway."

"You know more than you think you know," her grandmother insisted, not content with discussing paint. "You hire the right people and you start learning from those who know more than you do, people you trust." Gran smiled and handed Danny another cookie. "Besides, ranching's in your blood. You come from five generations of Texans, Katie. How many people can say that?"

"What's 'in your blood' mean?" the boy asked.

"It means you're born liking things your daddy likes," Gert replied. "And you've got a good daddy. Maybe you'll grow up to be a rancher, too."

Kate glanced toward Dustin, who was looking at her as if he wanted to get into a car and drive away someplace private and without deputy sheriffs with flashlights and attitudes. Well, there was a lot of land here on the Lazy K. If he wanted to be alone with her, all he had to do was open a car door and ask.

"I've got some cows to check on," the man said, serious as he could be though his dark eyes held a gleam that could only be described as X-rated. "Do you want to take a ride with me?"

Bingo.

"Go on," her grandmother said. "Danny and I will play a game of cards, won't we, boy?"

"Sure." He didn't even check with his father first, Kate noticed. The little kid really liked having Gert for a grandmother.

"Okay," Kate said, wondering if she should

sound so eager. It probably wasn't ladylike. "Let me get a hat."

"There's an extra in the truck." He stood and took his empty coffee cup to the sink. "We won't be gone more than an hour or two."

"I need to be back by five-thirty."

"There's no hurry," Gert said. "I'll call your mother and tell her we'll meet later, say about seven. Go on." She made a gesture as if shooing them out of the kitchen. "Go make my grand-daughter into a rancher," she told Dustin. "I could use some more help around here."

"You got me," Danny piped up. "I help."

"Yes, you sure do, honey, and—" her voice was drowned out by the squeak of the back door opening. Dustin put his hand on Kate's back and gently pushed her outside into the hot afternoon sun.

"I'd say we're going to be gone quite a while," the man declared.

"Look, Dustin, I—"

"Let's make your grandmother happy," he said. "And I wouldn't mind some cheering up myself."

"Is this about last night?"

"Forget about that," the man said, and Kate turned around to look up at him. "Let's go for a ride."

Forget about last night? Forget the way the cowboy's hands felt on her skin and what heated relief it was to sink against him and start making love?

Not likely.

HE TOLD HIMSELF he wanted to talk about the ranch, wanted to know where he stood should Gert move to town or—God forbid—die and leave the ranch to Jake and Kate. Jake would keep him on as foreman; he couldn't see the Johnsons moving off their own place and setting up housekeeping at the Lazy K. In a perfect world Kate would stay in New York and he would stay on as foreman, with free rein to improve the place, turn a profit and continue to run a few head of cattle himself.

In a perfect world, Kate would be naked and willing in his bed tonight, too.

She looked about twelve years old sitting beside him wearing a faded green baseball cap sporting the logo of Beauville Feed & Grain. He headed the truck north, with no particular destination in mind, except there was a pretty stand of cottonwoods by the creek up there. He decided there was only one way to deal with Kate McIntosh, and that was by making love to her. It was safe enough, he told himself. He was older and wiser. The boy who had promised "no strings" and gotten tangled up in love was now a grown man. A serious man with responsibilities and all sorts of experience. A man more than capable of protecting his heart against visiting city women.

But the rest of him wanted her. After all, here was Kate—long legs, gold-streaked hair, hazel eyes that with one look could make him hard. Could make him long for privacy and a long dark night to have her all to himself.

A hot bright afternoon would be the next best thing.

"Where are we going?"

He glanced toward her. "Do you care?" He dared her to protest, dared her to object.

"I suppose not." She stifled a yawn.

"Short night."

"Yes." She chuckled. "I think we'd better stay out of drive-ins from now on."

"Do you think that would solve this?"

"I don't think anything will, until I go back to New York."

"Out of sight, out of mind," he muttered, annoyed with the reminder of her other life. They rode in silence, as Dustin wondered if he'd made another mistake. He should have left her to paint the barn, should have spent his day far from any living creatures except for cattle.

But he wanted her. He hadn't slept much last night, knowing she was within walking distance.

He'd vowed to get her out of his system and then get on with his life, whatever it was he ended up doing. Fatherhood was going okay, even if he didn't have much experience at it. The boy seemed content enough with three meals a day and his own bed to sleep in.

Dustin parked the truck in the meager amount of shade a couple of scraggly trees provided. The brook was a mud puddle, and a couple of heifers eyed them from the other side of the sloping bank.

"Now what?" She turned to face him and he thought he saw her smile as if to tease. He didn't feel like smiling back.

"You're angry," she said. "Why?"

He could have told her then, he supposed. Explained he was angry that she'd believed some stupid rumors. Because she'd tossed him aside and all this time he'd thought it was because a wild Jones boy wasn't good enough for the honor student in the fancy home. She hadn't cared enough to ask him for the truth, hadn't loved him enough to suspect that there could have been an explanation, hadn't given him a chance to explain that he couldn't think of making love to someone else when Kate was in his life and in the back seat of his car.

"Sweetheart," he drawled. "Why would I be angry?" He was, though. It was old and went deep and he didn't like himself for holding on to it. He could tell her the truth any time he chose, but he didn't want to. Not yet. Let her think what she

wanted—she had for all these years, so what difference did it make now?

Dustin took a deep breath and looked out the
window. The heifers looked back at him as if they
too waited for the next move. He turned to face
her. "You kiss like a woman who hasn't been with
anyone for a long time."

"And you're an expert on women, of course,"
came the reply. She looked at him as if she was
trying to solve a puzzle. He didn't think she'd have
much luck.

"Of course."

"You act like a man who hasn't been with a
woman in a long time," she answered.

"And you would recognize the signs?" He
didn't want to think of the other men she'd slept
with. She was his—or she would be soon, if his
instincts were right—and that was all that mattered.

"Let's stop this," Kate said. "I don't want to
fight with you anymore."

"No," he agreed, taking his hands from the
steering wheel. His fingers were stiff. He turned
off the ignition and looked at her again. She took
off the cap and ran her fingers through her hair as
casually as if they were in the middle of a crowd.

"We can leave anytime," she said. "And we
can stay away from each other for the rest of my
vacation. It wouldn't be so hard to do."

"It would be impossible," Dustin said. "Gert is doing her best to throw us together."

"I can talk to her, get her to stop," Kate said.

"We came here to finish what we started last night," he reminded her, though the coward in him wanted her to fly back to New York this afternoon.

"Yes," she said, those hazel eyes studying him. "Do you think making love will help?"

"Couldn't hurt," he answered, as if discussing sex with her was effortless. His insides were re-arranging into knots.

"Oh, yes, it could," came her soft reply. Dustin wondered if she was finally being honest with him.

He reached for her, took her left hand and brought it to his mouth. He kissed her warm palm briefly. "I won't hurt you, Katie," he promised.

She was silent a moment.

"No strings?" Her question echoed his cocky declaration of years before. Her fingers swept his jaw and tempted him to kiss her.

"No strings," he agreed, though he knew as he spoke that he lied. He held her hand against his face for the length of a heartbeat and then, with his free hand, urged her closer. Her arms went to his shoulders, his hands cupped her face. The first kiss was light and sweet, a cautious brush of lips that tested his patience and teased his willpower.

He had neither. The next kiss, heated and in-tense, meant business. He wondered how he'd survived so long without kissing her, without moving his hands to the back of her head to hold her mouth against his. Kate moved closer, kneeling to meet him as she had so many other times before so that their lips would be level, so that she could slant her mouth and part her lips and take his tongue inside her mouth to tangle and mate with his.

He'd give all the cattle in Texas if he could keep kissing Kate McIntosh. It had been too long, a lifetime too long, since the last time he'd held her. Dustin managed to slide his hands to her back, skim her waist and dip under her T-shirt. Her skin was hot, reminding him of some pretty damn steamy nights in the drive-in. Reminding him of what it was like to be inside of her.

"Kate," he managed, lifting his mouth a scant inch from hers. His hands swept high under her shirt and touched the satiny fabric of her bra. "I don't want to do this on the front seat of the truck."

"No?" Her hands dropped to his chest and fumbled with the buttons of his denim work shirt.

"Not enough room," he managed to explain.

"I should have brought the Lincoln." She kissed the dimple in his chin. "Bigger back seat."

"Next time," he promised. The gods owed him this. Owed him time with the only woman he had ever fallen in love with. He wasn't in love with her now, of course—he was too smart for self-torture—but his physical reaction to her was the same as it had always been: pure unadulterated lust, the best of all feelings.

"Then where?"

"On the grass."

"Uh-uh," the lady said. "Rattlesnakes."

"The truck bed?"

She slipped the last button through its hole and skimmed her hands along his bare chest. "Too hard."

"I have a sleeping bag behind the seat." His hands moved higher, to cup her breasts, satin material covering what he wanted most to touch. It took only seconds to release the clasp so that those breasts spilled into his hands. Another practiced move and her shirt, along with her bra, ended up tossed over the gearshift.

"Works for me." Her bare breasts brushed his chest, her skin so hot and soft he thought he would explode right then and there. His hands rounded her shoulders, held her against him. "Still mad at me?"

"Yeah." His mouth found her neck, her collarbone, the little pulse there beating rapidly beneath his lips.

"I'm not too thrilled with you either," she murmured. Her hand found the waistband of his jeans and tugged on the snap.

"Wait," he managed to say, though the word

didn't come easy. He took a deep breath as he rested his forehead against hers. "If we don't slow down we will be doing it in the truck." It would be a bungled, hasty affair and not at all the stuff that fantasies were made of.

"Yes."

He lifted his hands and released her, but her eyes were closed and she didn't move right away. Dustin turned and fumbled behind the seat for the sleeping bag. "Come," he told her, and she opened her eyes and looked at him.

"We're crazy," was all she said.

"Yeah," he agreed, opening the door. "I know."

CHAPTER SIXTEEN

OF COURSE THIS WAS crazy, Kate decided, as Dustin disappeared from view. She was naked from the waist up in Dustin's truck. She was about to climb into the back of the truck and make love on a sleeping bag. It was the middle of the afternoon. A June afternoon in Texas. If the excitement didn't kill them, the heat surely would.

She was twenty-seven, not eighteen. But her age didn't have anything to do with falling in love. And falling in love she was, all over again. Or maybe she had never stopped. She'd been home for a handful of days and here she was, half-naked and aroused, waiting for Dustin to make a bed. Waiting for Dustin to make love to her.

Some things never changed.

"Kate?" He opened the truck door. His chest, browned and muscled, filled part of the opening. Dustin held out his hand and smiled at her. "I'm ready if you are." His gaze dropped to her bare breasts and then back to her face. "You're more beautiful than I remembered," he said.

Her heart flipped over when he looked at her like that. Her heart remembered a lot of things, she realized, as she took his hand. She grabbed her shirt and climbed out of the truck and took a breath of thick, heavy air. "Are you sure no one will come by?"

"I'm the only one who works this place, remember?"

"But it's not as if it was dark—"

He sat her on the open tailgate and stood in front of her. "No one is going to bother us, Katie, but if you want to leave, just say so."

She sat naked from the waist up and eyed Dustin's wide, bare chest. "I don't think I'm going anywhere."

"Well, that's a relief." He stepped forward, easily moving Kate's knees apart so he could stand closer to her. He took her crumpled blouse from her hand and once again tossed it aside. "You'd break my heart."

"I doubt that," she said, as he moved closer and ran his index finger down her breast.

"Why?" He didn't look at her, but bent to kiss her neck. His lips descended lower, to tease her peaked nipple with his tongue. Kate thought she might fall over, so she reached for him, held his shoulders, ran her fingers along his neck while he explored each breast and sent tingling warmth along her already sensitive skin.

She had no answer for him, of course. She couldn't think, especially when his hands found the waistband of her shorts and unzipped them. His fingers slipped underneath the elastic of her bikini underwear with tantalizing slowness, teasing her, and then returned to her waist.

Kate was lifted and set down in the middle of a fluffy blue sleeping bag, a place that looked like a virtual paradise compared to the front seat of the truck. It smelled of hay and horse, a combination she'd missed in New York. "You sleep here often?"

"Sometimes," he said, eyeing her as he climbed up and stretched out alongside her. "Alone."

She had no time to feel awkward, because Dustin reached over and lifted her on top of him. "There," he said with great satisfaction. "That's better."

She lay along the length of him, her breasts flat against his chest, her hair falling along his cheeks. She tucked it behind her ears so she could kiss him. He was hard against her thigh; she shifted so he pressed against the part of her that throbbed with anticipation.

"You're going to kill me," he said, playing with a strand of hair that dangled near his mouth.

"The sun might do that for me."

He shifted so they were on their sides, facing each other. "Better?"

"Mmm," she said, but not because she no longer felt the heat on her bare back, but because his hands were busy removing the rest of her clothing. She shifted to make it easier, wanting to feel the source of all that heat against her skin. Wanting him inside of her again, the way it used to be. They had never made love in the daylight before. She had never seen his body in other than shadows, in the light of the movie screen, and he had never seen hers.

His hands skimmed her bare thighs, the dip of her waist and back again, as if he wanted to give her time to get used to his touch. He tilted her slowly onto her back and then, with great speed, removed his clothing and returned to her.

Skin to skin was better, Kate concluded. Much better and infinitely more satisfying. She was wet and ready, though he took his time before entering her. Another difference, but not an unwelcome one. His hands were more knowing of a woman's body, his instincts honed. She took him in her arms and into her body and knew that somehow this was right and real and exactly what she wanted.

He filled her, inch by tantalizing inch, and smiled down into her eyes. "It's been a long time," he whispered, moving inside of her.

Too long, she would have replied, but he took her mouth and her breath and every vestige of control she clung to. He fit inside of her perfectly, as she remembered. And made love to her, as she remembered. And her body hadn't forgotten what it was like to tighten and climax around him. Her arms knew to hold him when he came deep inside of her, and her eyes sought his when it was over.

"I'm glad you're home," was all he said, before he kissed her again.

HE WAS IN DEEP TROUBLE.

No doubt about it, this Texan was out of his league. Dustin looked at himself in the cloudy mirror above the bathroom sink and saw a man who was hopelessly and foolishly and once again in love.

Nothing good could come of it. He rubbed shaving cream on his face and lifted his razor to the side of his face. He could end it all now and slit his throat, but Dustin Jones was no coward.

"Daddy?" The boy peered into the bathroom and a look of relief crossed his little face. The kid always looked like that whenever he saw his guardian, like he was surprised that Dustin was doing something normal. Like he was surprised that Dustin was around at all.

"What?" He continued to shave, rinsing the razor in the sink.

"Can I go to Grandma Gert's house tonight?"

"Why?"

The boy shrugged his skinny shoulders, trying to copy Dustin's familiar gesture. "'Cuz."

"Because why?"

Danny shrugged again, then scooted past Dustin to perch on the toilet seat lid.

"Sorry, pal. You'll have to do better than that." He continued to shave. "Besides, no one's home. The ladies have gone out to dinner."

"They have?"

"Yeah." Dustin splashed, making some shaving foam land on Danny's knee. He giggled and scooped it up with his finger, then leaned over and placed it on the back of Dustin's knee.

Dustin turned and pretended to growl with outrage, but the boy's eyes grew wide with fear and he scrambled to tuck himself into the small space behind the toilet.

Dustin tried to reassure him while he quickly cleaned up. He coaxed the boy from his hiding spot and settled him at the kitchen table.

"So I wouldn't get hit," Danny explained when Dustin asked him about his reaction. He still appeared wide-eyed, but was happy for chocolate milk and one of the cookies Gert had given him to take home. "It's a good place," he explained to his new father. "Mommy couldn't get me there."

Dustin managed to hold back his rage at this latest revelation. "Mommy" wasn't ever going to get her hands on this child again, not as long as

Dustin was there to protect the kid. He wished he could put the woman in jail, but a lawyer had already told him that was a waste of time. There'd been few charges against her, and the child abuse couldn't be proved. At least the boy was safe from his parents' destructive influence now. The court had put Lisa in a drug rehab center; Darrell was in prison and would be for another ten years. *Concentrate on the child,* the man had advised. *Make a home for him, so the judge will see he's being taken care of.*

"Does Kate have kids?"

"No." This afternoon he'd concentrated on making love to Kate. Not on work and not on the boy, but on Kate. He allowed himself to wonder what it would be like if she stayed on the ranch, if she took over from her grandmother. If she loved him back.

Oh, yeah. He'd fallen in love with her all over again, from the minute she'd walked into the grange hall in that fancy outfit and high-heeled shoes. Dustin grimaced, but the boy didn't see. He was busy picking chocolate chips out of the cookie and lining them up on the table. For some reason that was big entertainment.

"Why not?"

"Why not what?" He opened the refrigerator and took out some eggs and bacon. Surely there was nothing wrong with eating breakfast for supper.

"Why doesn't Kate have kids? Doesn't she like kids?"

"I'm sure she does," Dustin replied. She seemed happy enough to baby-sit the Bennett kids yesterday. And she was kind to Danny, even though she thought he was the reason she and Dustin had broken up.

"Does she like *me?*" Now the chocolate chips were shoved into a pile, readied to be eaten all at once, Dustin supposed.

"Sure she does."

He should tell her the truth, but would it make any difference? It may have been nine years ago, but the truth wasn't going to change anything now. Let the woman think what she wanted. She would be gone in nine days and he doubted she would stay if he asked her. He didn't have much to offer a woman who already had everything.

But in his heart he knew Kate belonged here, belonged here with him and the boy.

Too bad Kate was the only one who didn't seem to realize it.

"I REALIZE YOU DON'T approve, Martha, but I have to think of my career." Gert shuffled through the stacks of papers spread over the kitchen table.

"Now where did I put those pictures of my mother and father?"

"Your career," Martha repeated, praying for patience. If her mother was really delusional, she was going to need all the patience God could send her way. "You haven't written the book yet, Mother. Maybe you should wait until you've finished it before you give interviews to—"

"I'm ninety," Gert snapped, fussing through a stack of old photographs. "How much longer do you think I should wait?"

Until hell freezes over and the cows come home, Martha wanted to say. Until it snows in July and Texans quit drinking beer. She looked at her watch and realized she had little time to spend arguing with her mother over a newspaper interview. She'd come out to the ranch to see Kate, but the girl had gone off somewhere with Dustin and the boy again. "When's Kate coming back?"

"I didn't ask."

Martha tried another tactic. "You know, Mother, it's a wonderful idea to write the family history, but don't you think telling stories about the folks around here might be considered an...invasion of privacy?"

Gert snorted. "History's history. No one can change it, no matter how much they want to."

Well, that was true. Martha thought of things she'd change and things she wouldn't. Mostly she'd do things a lot smarter if she could do them over again. It was too bad she wouldn't get the chance.

She eyed the piles of papers on the table. With any luck, Gert would lose interest before it was done. "I'll be out tomorrow. Did you write down a grocery list?"

"Kate did." Gert waved in the direction of the refrigerator, so Martha walked across the kitchen and found the list underneath a magnet shaped like Texas. "You have a date tonight, Mattie?"

"As a matter of fact, I do," she admitted. "Carl is taking me to Marysville for the Friday night seafood special at Lou Lou's."

"I'm glad you're getting out."

"It's nice to have a man around," Martha said, which had to be the understatement of the summer. She had plans for tonight that had more excitement than the Super Shrimp Platter. She looked out the window in time to see Dustin's truck, in a cloud of dust, arrive out back. "Here's Kate. Do you think she's serious about him?"

"I hope so," Gert said, joining her at the window. "I'd like to think she's as smart as I think she is."

"That young man is trouble," Martha muttered. "I just know it."

"Kate can take care of herself," Gert declared. "The women in our family are good at that."

"Yes," she agreed, but grudgingly. "Just be careful what you say to that reporter today. You don't want folks getting all riled up."

"I'll be fine. I'm gonna give 'em enough to whet their appetite, that's all."

"Fine," Martha said, knowing full well her mother would say whatever she wanted to say. She glanced at her watch again. She was getting her hair done at two, her nails at three and she still had to change the sheets on her bed and clean the bathroom before she headed to the beauty parlor. Tonight was the night to add a little romance into her own life.

For the rest of this Friday she would pretend that her mother wasn't going to air the town's dirty linen and that her daughter wasn't having an affair with the hired help. Besides, the construction of the Good Night Villas had progressed nicely, which meant there were some secrets in town that would remain buried.

SURELY SHE COULD keep her jeans on tonight, Kate decided, looking at herself in the full-length mirror in the upstairs bedroom she'd claimed as her own this vacation. The red heels could be a little much, but the sleeveless red top with its pearl snaps and demure fringe was perfect for dancing.

Perfect for driving her cowboy crazy, which was the real point, she knew, despite her good intentions. She wanted to look so damn good that the man would take her home early and make love to her all night.

Which would be a dumb thing to do.

Kate kicked off the heels and eyed her sandals. If she wore a long-sleeved denim shirt over a white tank, she would look sporty. If she went with red, she would look like she was asking for sex.

And of course she was, but she didn't have to be obvious about it. They hadn't made love since the time in the truck on Tuesday. So obviously she did have to be obvious, or else she'd be forced to conclude that Dustin had gotten her out of his system.

She hated to think that. Like she hated to think she was falling in love with him again. Like she hated to think the man would *know* she was falling in love with him again. Really, she wasn't sure which was worse.

Kate put the red heels back on and prepared to torture the man. It was the least she could do when, for the past three days, he'd acted as if they'd never made love. A woman had her pride.

CHAPTER SEVENTEEN

THE LAST CHANCE SALOON would never be the same. Dustin figured from the admiring looks that were coming Kate's way that he'd be lucky if he didn't get into a fight before the night was over. Protecting the lady's honor could get difficult. Wearing that outfit—snug blue jeans, fancy red shoes and a top that fit her curves a little too well— Kate attracted a lot of attention. Oh, there were other pretty women showing more skin and wearing tighter clothing, but none were as beautiful as Kate.

And there were none that could cause his heart to settle in his throat every time he looked at her. Dustin guided his date through the crowd at the bar and managed to find a small table in the back corner. Friday night in Beauville was almost as big a party night as Saturday night in Beauville.

"You wore that outfit on purpose, right? To torture me?" He pulled out a wooden chair for her and caught a whiff of her perfume as she sat down.

"Of course."

"That's what I thought. Why?" He took the chair closest to her and angled himself so that no one could approach them easily. Kate had the nerve to smile at him.

"To get your undivided attention."

"You have it." His gaze dropped to the snaps on her blouse. "Those aren't going to come undone while you're dancing, right?"

"I hope not."

Dustin wasn't so sure she wore a bra underneath that red shirt. He frowned. "Don't dance with anyone but me."

"I never intended to."

He looked around, glared at a couple of young cowboys and turned back to Kate. "Maybe this wasn't such a good idea."

"You can't get out of it now," she said. "I asked you to go dancing and you said yes."

He would have said yes to anything she asked. He'd watched her paint the barn, he'd taken her along in his truck when he'd gone to town, he'd been careful never to be alone with her, but a man could only take so much torture before he broke down and agreed to dance. Agreed to take the woman he loved into his arms and hold her while the band played something slow. "Buckle bumping" music, Bobby Calhoun had called it.

"I'm not much of a dancer," Dustin warned, wondering how long they would have to stay at

the Last Chance before he could take her home to
bed. Danny was staying with Gert, so the bunkhouse would be empty. If they didn't turn on any
lights neither Gert nor Danny would have to know
they were there.

"I'll take my chances." Kate didn't look at all
concerned. She also didn't look as if she had
thought much beyond simply going dancing with
him, though she'd admitted to wearing that outfit
to make him crazy.

"I'll go get us a drink," he said, torn between
staying at the table to keep predatory cowboys
away from her and getting some distance so he
wouldn't make a fool of himself by hauling her
out of the bar and into his truck within the next
ten minutes. "What do you want?"

"Beer is fine." She tapped her fingers in time
to the band's rendition of Clint Black's latest hit
and looked out at the dance floor.

"I'll be right back," he said, hesitating before
he left the table. "Don't go anywhere."

"I won't," she promised. Once again she
smiled, and Dustin knew he couldn't possibly let
her go back to New York without a fight.

"I mean it," he said, this time he held her gaze
until she realized he wasn't talking about leaving
the table. The smile disappeared from her face.
"Don't go, Katie."

"My job—"

"Could be running a ranch," he finished for her. *With me,* he wanted to add. He placed his palms flat on the table and leaned toward her. He wanted her to be able to hear despite the music. "Do you love it? Your job, I mean?"

She hedged. "Am I supposed to?"

"If you choose New York instead of Texas, yes." He waited a moment for her to answer. Then, figuring he'd given her something to think about, he turned and headed toward the bar.

Tonight he would tell her the truth. He would ask her to stay, to give him a chance to prove to her that she belonged here in Texas, that she belonged here with him. But would she want the boy? Would she want to trade New York glamour for Texas dust?

Dustin bought a couple of beers, greeted some friends, avoided flirting smiles of one of the Wynette twins—he never could tell those girls apart—and headed back to Kate. Would she marry him if he asked her?

He almost dropped one of the beer bottles. Marriage hadn't been in his plans, but loving Kate for the rest of his life looked like a sure thing. Now that he'd lost his heart, he was in too deep to turn back, whether Kate agreed to a wedding or not.

KATE WANTED TO DANCE. Right now she didn't want to think about returning to New York. She hadn't wanted to answer the harried phone calls from her boss and the e-mails from the producer about changes to the mystery baby story line. She'd grown tired of mystery baby story lines, demanding producers and a sponsor who wanted high ratings and no excuses. For now Kate wanted to paint the barn and listen to Gran's stories and mend fence and be worshipped by a little boy and made love to by the only man she'd ever been in love with. She didn't want to think about the future and she didn't want to think about *Loves of Our Lives* or who would be fired after the November ratings sweeps.

Uncharacteristic, true, but then wasn't a woman entitled to a vacation? Especially when a handsome cowboy took her in his arms and two-stepped across the scarred wooden dance floor?

"Nice," she murmured. Dustin's neck smelled wonderful, like spice and leather. He held her tighter, which raised her temperature a few degrees. Dancing was wonderful, but going home should be even better.

"How much longer?" he asked, his hands firmly holding her waist as they rocked to "The Dance."

"Until what?"

"Until we're alone." The music ended, but Dustin didn't release her. They weren't the only ones still embracing on the dance floor; it was close to midnight, so more than a handful of couples had romance on their minds.

"How long does it take to get back to the Lazy K?"

"Too long," he muttered, "but I'll drive as fast as I can."

"Good idea," she said, as he released her and, grabbing her hand, tugged her toward the door.

"Let's go," he said, and Kate hurried to keep up. She liked a man who knew what he wanted. As long as he didn't ask her to stay in Texas again, it would be a wonderful evening.

MARTHA DIDN'T EXPECT him to spend the night. Actually, she thought, carefully slipping out of her double bed so she wouldn't wake her date, she hadn't thought much beyond the lovemaking.

It had been fine and dandy, just not as exciting as she'd hoped. And went on a little too long, too, if the truth be told. She wasn't one to complain. She'd just thought it would be a bit more romantic. Like the movies.

But she wasn't the virginal bride on her honeymoon and Carl wasn't a dashing husband. He was a good friend and a fun companion, and that was the most anyone could expect at sixty-four.

Martha took a shower with the bathroom door locked. It made her a little nervous having Carl in the house at seven in the morning. And his car was still parked out front. She'd wanted some excitement, she reminded herself as she donned a full-length bathrobe and tiptoed into her bedroom for something to wear. But she hadn't intended to be a source of neighborhood gossip. Next time—if there was a next time—she'd make sure he parked his car in the garage while she parked hers in the driveway. Or maybe they'd just use her car, which would be easier. Or go to his apartment—which, come to think of it, she didn't want to do at all. She didn't think she wanted to wake up in a strange bed, in a strange room. She needed her bathroom, her makeup, her magnifying mirror.

"Martha?"

She froze, her clothing clutched to her chest. "Yes?"

"Good morning." Carl fumbled with the covers and sat up. He smiled at her and patted her side of the bed. "Come back to bed, sweetie?"

"I just took a shower," she said, knowing darn well what was in store if she got back in that bed. She'd rather have a good cup of coffee. "I have to dry my hair and—"

"Later. There's something here that can't wait."

"Oh, I'll bet it can," she insisted. "Hold that thought and I'll be back in a few minutes." She locked herself in the bathroom again in order to dress, blow-dry her hair into waves and put on her makeup. With any luck she could get downstairs and put the coffee on before Carl became any more amorous. Really, she wasn't sure men were worth all this trouble.

"Martha?"

"I'll be right back," she promised, once she was out of the bathroom again. "I'll put the coffee on and get the paper."

"We can read it in bed together," he said, looking pleased. Martha smiled at him. She supposed the man got lonely, too. And it *was* nice to have company at breakfast. She wasn't about to take her clothes off and climb into bed in broad daylight, though.

A woman had to set some ground rules.

DUSTIN WOULD HAVE liked to spend the night with her. Would have preferred to wake up and find Kate asleep in his bed instead of the boy.

Danny was spread out on his back, his bony arms and legs sprawled in all directions. He needed a haircut and there was chocolate on his chin. He and Grandma Gert must have eaten cookies all evening. Well, that was okay. At least he hoped it was. He'd heard that grandparents liked to do things like that, and Gert was the closest thing to a grandmother the boy would ever have.

Dustin slid out of bed, the bed that had a few hours earlier held him and Kate. They'd never made love in a bed before, so he was lucky he hadn't had a heart attack from sheer happiness. By the time it was over he'd lost the power to speak, so discussing Danny's parentage hadn't been a topic of conversation, though he knew he had to tell her the truth soon. He'd only been capable of a couple of soft groans as he'd tucked Kate's naked body against his and covered them with a sheet.

They'd had time for a short nap before heading over to Gert's and pretending they'd just closed down the Last Chance. He'd gathered up Danny, asleep on Gert's couch, and left Gert working on her book and Kate looking a little dazed. He knew how she felt.

Dustin threw on his work clothes and headed out to do chores. Later on he'd clean up and see if Kate was free for breakfast. It was long past time for some serious conversation.

It was long past time to tell her he loved her.

"MOTHER, I CAN'T BELIEVE you did this!"

Gert finished fixing the coffeemaker and turned it on before giving her daughter her attention. It was a little early in the morning for one of Martha's indignations. "Good morning to you, too, Martha. The coffee will be ready in a few minutes."

"I'm not here about coffee," she said, placing a copy of the Beauville paper on the kitchen table. It was folded so that Gert could see a photo of herself as a young girl on the front page. "I'm here about *this*."

"I was a looker, wasn't I," Gert murmured. "Did this come out this morning?"

"Yes, unfortunately."

"Martha, what are you so worked up about?" Gert adjusted her glasses and studied the article. The young man had done a good job, except he'd described her as "wrinkled." She wasn't sure he needed to use that word. She preferred "mature." She'd have to inform him of that next time, when the book came out or when she sold the movie rights. She'd heard about movie deals on that television show, *Entertainment Tonight*. What she needed was one of those theatrical agents. Kate would know.

Martha took the paper out of her hands and read, "'Gert's family owned several ranches in this area during the eighteen hundreds, including land north of town where the Good Night Villas are under construction, which was originally the ranch of cattleman Horace Stewart, Mrs. Knepper's great-grandfather.'"

"That's not exactly something to get worked up over," Gert declared. "Horace Stewart was a fine man. Told stories about the winter of the Big Drift, back in 1865, that would curl your toes."

Kate, in a T-shirt and shorts, entered the room

and yawned. "What's going on? I could hear you upstairs."

"Your mother is in a snit about something," Gert said.

"Hi, Mom." She padded over and kissed them both, then headed toward the coffeepot.

"I just turned it on," Gert said. "You'll have to give it a minute."

"Okay."

Gert turned her attention back to her daughter, whose hair looked mussed. It wasn't like Martha to have mussed hair. "What did you do to your hair this morning?"

"Never mind my hair," she said, looking a little embarrassed. She started reading again, "'Mrs. Knepper tells tales of cattle rustling, wagon trains, range wars and family feuds. I hope when she finishes writing her story, she'll tell us if the missing shipment of gold is really buried on her great-grandfather's ranch, as outlaw Dead-Eye Dan claimed it was before the noose finished his life of crime forever.'"

Gert grinned. "That'll make 'em all go out and buy copies of the book, won't it?"

"You never mentioned missing gold, Gran." Kate handed her a cup of coffee, so Gert sat down and dumped some cream and sugar in it. She didn't know why Martha was making a big deal out of this.

"My grandfather used to tell that story, not that anyone believed him, but I thought it would make good reading—Martha, whatever is the matter with you?" Her daughter had gone pale and sank into a chair. "Better put your head down between your legs."

"Mother?"

"I'll be all right," she said, her voice a little muffled in her cotton skirt. "Give me a minute."

"Too much excitement," Gert declared. "I don't think dating that Jackson man is a good idea."

"—not his fault," Martha muttered.

Gert winked at Kate. "Are you having one of them menopausal fits again?"

"That was over ten years ago." Martha raised her head and looked like she was going to cry, so Gert quit teasing and drank some coffee instead while Kate handed her mother a cold washcloth.

"Thank you," Martha sniffed. "Honestly, I don't know what I'm going to do with you."

"Both of us or just Gran?"

"Both of you, I suppose," Martha said, leaning back in her chair. "You're sleeping with that cowboy and your grandmother is destroying my life."

"You're sleeping with him?" Gert turned to Kate. "Well, thank goodness. I thought you'd never come to your senses. I'll have to call my lawyer Monday."

"Why?"

"Yes," Martha asked. "Why?"

Gert decided that neither one of them needed to know the details. "Never mind that," she said. "How could I possibly be destroying your life, Mattie?"

"Everyone's going to start hunting for gold at the drive-in now."

"Oh, Carl won't mind. He'll figure it's good publicity," Gert said. She saw Dustin approach the screen door and waved him inside.

"Of course," Kate agreed, patting her mother's shoulder. "And he has security guards there, remember? I'm sure he won't be angry about it."

Her gray-haired daughter, the perfect child who had never done a thing wrong in her entire life, took a deep breath and said, "There's a dead body at the drive-in and I don't want anyone to find it."

Gert choked on her coffee. "Carl's *dead?*"

"Have you called the sheriff—what's his name, Gran?"

"Sheridan," Dustin said, entering the kitchen. "Jess Sheridan."

"How did it happen?" Kate asked. "Did the poor man have a heart attack or something?"

Martha took a deep breath. "Carl is very much alive, thank you. We were having breakfast together—" She paused, blushed and then continued. "We were having breakfast together when I read the article about your grandmother. After I threw up, I got in the car and came out here.''

''Martha.'' Gert had never seen her daughter so upset. ''Who's dead at the drive-in?''

''I can't tell you that.'' She put her head down on the kitchen table and started to cry.

Gert leaned close to her. ''You can't or you won't?''

Martha only cried harder. Kate turned to Dustin and offered him coffee, but he declined.

''I didn't mean to interrupt a family discussion,'' he said.

''We could use some advice.'' Gert pointed to an empty chair. ''Sit down. As soon as she stops crying we're going to need a man's opinion.'' And maybe someone good with a shovel. And if Dustin was sleeping with her granddaughter and going to become a member of the family, he might as well know all the family secrets sooner rather than later.

CHAPTER EIGHTEEN

DUSTIN FIGURED HE wasn't going to get the chance to talk to Kate this morning. Her mother was still crying, her grandmother continued to demand answers and got none, while Kate handed her mother tissues and drank coffee as if her sanity depended on it.

Dustin decided to pour himself a cup and wished he hadn't picked this time to see if Kate was awake and ready for serious conversation. He didn't figure Martha for a murderer, couldn't figure out why she'd know about a body in the drive-in and certainly didn't want to contemplate the reason why the woman had been having breakfast so early on a Saturday morning with Carl Jackson.

Clearly there was a lot going on here that he didn't understand, so Dustin gestured to Kate the next time she glanced his way.

"We'll be right back," he told Gert, and took Kate's hand.

"Don't go far," the old lady replied. "She'll

have to stop crying soon and then we'll get some answers.''

"Right.'' He hauled Kate outside and around the corner of the house, in the shade of the overhang. First he kissed her, and was glad to note that she kissed him back.

"Good morning,'' she said, smiling up at him.

"I missed you.''

"I know.'' Her smile faded. "I wanted to wake up with you and instead—do you think my mother is having a nervous breakdown?''

"Does she cry like that a lot?''

"Never. Not since Daddy died.'' She lowered her voice, though Dustin was certain neither Gert nor Martha could hear. "But this talk about a dead body really seems strange. If she knew there was someone dead there, why would she want to buy one of the villas and move in?''

"Maybe she just discovered it.''

"My mother? Discovering dead bodies?'' Kate shook her head. "Bargains, yes. Bodies, no.''

"Kate, honey, how did all this start?''

"Mom was upset because Gran told the reporter about some buried treasure rumored to be hidden at the drive-in. Supposedly Gran's great-grandfather lived on a ranch there at the time and told her the story. She thought it would make her book more interesting.''

It had certainly made his morning more interesting, though he would have preferred waking up naked and next to Kate. That would have been interesting enough. "All I heard was the part about not wanting anyone to find 'the body.'"

"We should call the sheriff."

"Not so fast," Dustin warned. "If your mother isn't, uh, in her right mind, you don't want to make things worse."

"Maybe we should call a lawyer, or a doctor."

"Your mother can't cry forever," he said, hoping he was right. "Give her a chance to explain before you call for reinforcements."

She sighed. "You're right." Kate stood on tiptoe and kissed him lightly. "Where's Danny?"

"Still sleeping. Gert wore him out last night. I think they watched movies 'til midnight."

"Figures. She likes the company."

"Me, too." They smiled at each other for a long moment.

"I was going to go see Emily today and take her some groceries. I'm not sure if I can do that now. But if I go, do you think Danny would like to ride along?"

"I think he'd like that a lot. He has a crush on you, you know."

"I've noticed. He's a nice kid, Dustin," she told him.

"Yeah," he said, before kissing her again. "I know."

"I'd better get back," she said, pulling away. "Do you think maybe Mom was involved in a hit-and-run accident last night?"

"I can't see your mother doing anything illegal," he assured her, but over the top of Kate's head he saw the sheriff's car pull up in the drive. "Kate?"

"What?"

"Maybe you'd better go tell your mother that the sheriff is coming."

"Oh, my God," she breathed, peering around him. "He's going to arrest her."

"I doubt it," Dustin said, setting her away from him and turning her toward the kitchen door. "Go. I'll see what he wants."

He made sure she went inside before heading toward Jess Sheridan, who had just stepped out of his car. "Jess? Hey."

"Hey, Dustin," the man said, settling his hat on his head. "It's going to be another hot one."

"Yeah, it sure is." He shook the man's hand and waited for the reason he was here, knowing Sheridan would get around to it in his own time.

"I could have called," Jess said, "but I was out this direction anyway." He looked around. "Where's the boy?"

"Still asleep."

"Good. I wanted to tell you that Lisa is out of jail, as of yesterday. She supposedly completed a drug treatment program and got time off for good behavior.''

Dustin felt like someone had punched him in the gut. ''Where is she?''

''I don't know. That's why I thought you should know.''

''Thanks.''

''You've got custody, right?''

''Yeah, so far. We go to court again in September.''

Jess nodded and opened the car door. ''Good. Take care of the boy and call me if there's any problem.''

''Thanks.'' He watched the sheriff put the car in reverse and turn around before heading back to the road. Jess Sheridan hadn't brought good news, but at least he hadn't arrested Dustin's future mother-in-law.

''IT WAS JUST A NIGHTMARE.'' Martha sniffed and tossed a large handful of tissues into the trash. ''I guess I just had a bad dream.''

''You expect us to believe that?'' Kate crossed her arms over her chest and thought once again about calling a doctor, preferably one who carried sedatives around with him. ''After crying for half an hour about a body at the drive-in and how gold hunters might find it?''

''It was quite a nightmare, I must say,'' her

mother declared. She reached into her purse and found her lipstick. "Excuse me. I'm going to go freshen up."

Kate watched as her mother left the room and headed around the corner for the bathroom. "What do you think, Gran?"

"I think we're lucky the sheriff didn't come into the house," her grandmother said. "There's no telling what Martha might have told him."

Kate reheated her coffee in the microwave and then sat down at the kitchen table. "What do you think she was talking about?"

"I'm not sure," her grandmother said, but she avoided Kate's gaze and instead went over to the window. "Looks like Dustin's working on the roof. That man is always working."

Kate wondered if he had his shirt off. If he was thinking of last night. Or planning how they would be together tonight. "Maybe I should take Mom home. She isn't in any condition to drive."

"I'm going to sell him the ranch, Kate." Gert left the window and shuffled over to the table and sat down. "If you don't want the Lazy K, that's what I'm going to do."

"Gran—"

"Don't say anything now," her grandmother told her. "You have another week here to think about what you want to do, but I can't run this place much longer. It needs a man and it looks like it's got one, so I might as well make it official.''

Kate took a deep breath. She'd never thought the ranch would leave the family. "I don't think Dustin can afford to buy a ranch, Gran. And where will you live? Certainly not in the Good Night Villas with Mom?"

"I'll make Dustin a good deal. Lord knows neither you nor Jake needs money. Jake has his own place free and clear and you have your fancy career. Your mother is fixed just fine for money, with or without the Lazy K so it's not like we're gonna go broke."

"No," Kate said, feeling as if she was going to lose something she didn't know she wanted so much. "I guess not."

"It's yours, though," her grandmother said, "if you want to stay."

"What is?" Martha said, entering the room. "Are you trying to bribe Kate with this ranch again, Mother?"

"I'm not discussing my business with a crazy woman, Martha," Gert declared. "Are you feeling better?"

"I am," she said. Kate saw that her mother had combed her hair and put on lipstick. Her eyes were still red and puffy, but at least she wasn't crying anymore.

"So, who's in the drive-in?"

"Don't start, Mother."

Kate frowned at her grandmother, then took her mother's arm. "Let me drive you home. I'd planned on visiting with Emily for a while this morning."

"I'm perfectly capable of taking myself home. Besides, I'm playing bridge with the girls this afternoon." She avoided looking at either one of them and fussed with her blouse, making sure it was tucked neatly into her skirt.

"Do you want to come out here for dinner tonight?"

"No, thank you, dear," Martha said. She dropped her lipstick into her purse and snapped it shut. "I think I'll go to bed early tonight. I could use the rest."

"Hmph," Gert said, looking worried. "I should say so."

Kate walked her mother to her car, but Martha didn't say a word until she got behind the wheel. "I'm sorry I frightened you."

"Are you sure you're okay?"

"Of course," she said, but to Kate she looked ten years older than she had yesterday. "I just need some time to rest. That article in the paper just…upset me, that's all."

"Gran's book has upset you from the beginning," Kate said, leaning down so she could look through the open car window. Her mother's fingers

gripped the steering wheel, but she didn't say anything. Instead she fussed with her keys and started
the car, so Kate had no choice but to back away
and let her mother leave the ranch.

It was one of those mornings she should have
stayed in bed—with Dustin. Dead bodies, gold
hunters, sheriffs, hysterical mothers and career de-
cisions would have been ignored, at least until after
she'd rolled on top of his naked body and had her
way with him.

SHE WOULD NOT MAKE that mistake again, Martha
decided. At first she'd thought that newspaper article was the last straw, that there was nothing to
do but to come clean and confess everything.

And then she'd seen her mother's face. How
could she tell her ninety-year-old mother the truth?
Gert couldn't live forever. Let her find out in
heaven, when some nice angels would gather
around her and explain everything. That would certainly be much easier than hearing it this way.

And the mess that would follow couldn't be
helped. There were a few people around town who
would remember and understand, but there were
lots more who would judge without knowing what
it was really like to have a best friend.

A best friend was someone you would do anything for.

"YOUR LIFE IS SO much more exciting than mine," Emily declared, tucking her baby to her breast.

"I guess that depends on how you define 'exciting.'" Kate suffered another unfamiliar twinge of envy as she watched Emily feed her baby. "I thought I was coming home for a peaceful vacation with my family."

"And instead?" Emily's face took on that expression of blissful contentment as the baby began to nurse. "An affair with your grandmother's foreman, a mysterious dead body and a grandmother trying to get famous."

"Exactly. I should be writing all of this down for the show. My boss would love the 'mysterious dead body' part."

"I personally prefer the romance," her friend said. "I'm glad you brought Danny with you. John could use some male company."

"I'll take him back to the ranch with me for the afternoon, okay?"

"You have to ask?" Emily laughed. "My mother's taking the girls with her to Marysville, so that will work out great. I hate to ask this, but when do you have to go back to New York?"

"Next Saturday. I could make my boss happy and leave the day after tomorrow, but I won't."

"You can't leave now," Emily said, "not until you decide what to do about your mother, never mind the ranch and Dustin. And you promised to go out to lunch with Elizabeth and Lorna, too, re-member?''

She remembered. And looked forward to it, too, though she didn't really think she'd fit in.

''If I stayed,'' Kate said, thinking out loud, ''I'd live with my grandmother out on the ranch. With Dustin so close, I'm not sure if that's a good idea or not. If he started dating someone else, it would be messy. And if I started dating someone else, it would be even messier.''

''You're not ready to admit that he's the one man for you, huh?'' Emily shook her head. ''I can't believe it.''

''He slept with someone else and made a baby while he was going out with me,'' Kate reminded her. ''He might not make the best husband.''

''That's history. He's a responsible father now. People change. And people grow up. Look, you could buy your mother's house and live here in town.''

''By myself in a house with four bedrooms? The place is huge.''

''It's the nicest house in town. Forget the past. Marry Dustin and fill it up with kids.''

''He hasn't asked.'' She watched Emily lift the tiny baby to her shoulder to burp her. ''And what would I do here in Beauville?''

''Run the ranch. You've always loved that place.

I assume you have some money saved so you could afford to get it going again?''

"Yes," she said, thinking of her hefty savings account. She'd never been a big spender, having learned frugal ways from Gert, and writing for daytime television was a lucrative career. "When I was eighteen that was all I wanted, Dustin Jones and the Lazy K. Makes me wish I hadn't grown up," she admitted, watching Emily comfort her fussing baby. "Can I hold her?"

"If you don't mind if she spits up on your clothes." Emily leaned over and tucked the baby, bundled in soft cotton, into Kate's arms.

"I don't mind." She kept her voice quiet, as the baby's eyelids closed. Her little lips pursed, as if she wondered where her lunch disappeared to. "You make all of this look so easy, Em."

"It's hard work—don't let anyone tell you different," Emily drawled. "But first, Kate, you have to decide what you want. If it's that big career, then run—don't walk—to the airport before you start breaking hearts."

"And if it's Dustin and the ranch?"

"The two go together?"

"I think so."

"Then tell him you're thinking about staying and see what happens."

"You make it sound so easy." She could hold this baby all day long, Kate decided. It was too bad she had a barn to paint and her grandmother's latest chapters to read, a mystery to solve and a mother to comfort—plus a man to love and his son to care for.

"It is easy," Emily insisted, struggling off the couch. "You sit there and rock the baby while I go clean up, then we'll plan your future."

"Okay," Kate agreed, inhaling the sweet scent of baby as she lifted her closer. "You win. I want one of these."

"Don't tell me," Emily said. "Tell that cowboy of yours."

"He's not 'my cowboy.'"

Emily laughed. "Sure he is. You're the only person in town who doesn't know it."

There was a lot she didn't know, Kate mused, rocking slowly so the baby would sleep. She didn't know if Dustin loved her, didn't know whether or not she should take over the ranch, and certainly didn't know whose body was buried at the former Good Night Drive-In.

But she did know she was in love. That was something to think about.

CHAPTER NINETEEN

GERT DIDN'T UNDERSTAND what all the fuss was about, but it boded well for the success of her book. Seemed like everyone in town wanted to know what she was writing about or if she knew the location of the gold—as if she'd tell if she did—and did Gert need any more stories or photos because so-and-so was going through her mother's things and there was quite a bit of information there. The Jeffersons were upset, since they didn't want anyone knowing their great-great-grandfather had come to town when he jumped off a train, having escaped a murder conviction in California. And Irene Gardiner wanted to make sure that no one found out her mother was illegitimate. The phone rang a lot more than it ever had, not that she had to answer it. Kate did that for her.

Kate did a lot of things that helped Gert spend more time writing. She made coffee and cleaned. She cooked and shopped and proofread each chapter of the manuscript.

"You're a good girl," Gert told her. "I don't

know what I would do without you." It was a pretty big hint, but Gert didn't care. When a person was as old as she was, she was allowed to say anything.

So she said things like, "You'd have to go a long way to find a man as good as Dustin Jones" and "I hope I see your children before I die." Sentiments like that were bound to make the girl think twice about leaving for New York.

The boy came around, too. He and Gert drank coffee milk and ate cookies. Gert promised to make cinnamon rolls as soon as her book was done because she had no time for baking now. She was in the 1960s already, so it wouldn't be long before the book was done. She hadn't much cared for the sixties—except for Martha's wedding in 1969—so she didn't intend to dwell on much of it. There were some things worth skipping over, some things just too painful to write about.

"Gran?" Kate stood in the entrance to the living room. "Do you want to take a break for lunch?"

"No, thanks, dear. You and Danny go ahead without me." She wanted to finish this section before she stopped for a sandwich and a nap. Besides, Kate needed to get used to being with the boy. She would make a good mother, that girl would. Gert could see them from where she sat. Danny never strayed far from Kate's side, which was good. Dustin would be in soon, too, since he'd taken to eating lunch in the main house.

Kate was getting real good at fixing lunches, and painting outbuildings. And Gert had heard her talking to Dustin about cattle prices and land management. Danny started talking about getting his own horse and Emily's little boy had been over to play three times in three days. Jake and Elizabeth were bringing the new baby over to visit tomorrow.

Yes, Gert thought, going back to her memories of the 1960s. Everyone was acting like one big happy family. Everyone but Martha, who refused to talk about her mother's book except to beg her to stop working on it.

"ARE YOU SURE YOU don't mind?" Dustin hesitated at the kitchen door. "I'm not going to be back from Marysville until evening. There's no knowing how long these stock auctions will last."

"It's okay," Kate said, though she wasn't sure what she would do with an eight-year-old boy for the entire day. Danny was quiet enough, but there seemed to be a lot going on behind those serious brown eyes. She'd give a lot to know what the boy was thinking, especially when she caught him staring at her.

"Tomorrow's Friday," Dustin said. He lifted her chin with his index finger. "We have a date?"

"We'd better," she said. "We haven't been alone in a long time."

"Between grandmothers and kids, it's not easy," the man agreed, then brushed a kiss across her mouth.

"Maybe we should sneak off to the hayloft tonight." There hadn't been much chance to be alone with him. Gert was typing and Danny was gathering his trucks together to play with by the back door, which meant Kate could at least get a few kisses.

"I can't ask Gert to baby-sit Danny so her foreman can have sex with her granddaughter."

"I guess not." Kate sighed. "But you have to admit it's tempting."

"Tomorrow night," he promised. "Let's go out to dinner, just the two of us. We haven't had much time to be alone this week," he said, voicing her thoughts.

"I'd like that."

"Okay." The next kiss lasted much longer, until Kate's knees turned weak and she wondered how on earth she could wait until tomorrow night before being alone with him. The only reason they stopped was because they heard Danny singing as he came around the corner of the house.

"Gotta go." Dustin released her, then called goodbye to his son. "Be good," he reminded the child.

"You're coming back, right?" the boy asked.

"Yeah. After I buy some cattle, and maybe a horse or two."

"I can't come?"

"It's too long a day, pal," Dustin said, giving the kid a hug around his skinny shoulders. "And you have to be a little older before you can go. I think you'll have a better time here with Kate and Grandma Gert."

"Kate could go with us," Danny said, obviously unwilling to let his father out of his sight.

"I can't," Kate answered. "I promised Gran I'd make fried chicken for dinner tonight. And I bought all the stuff to make homemade ice cream." She almost laughed at the expression on Danny's face. Fried chicken and ice cream made up for missing an auction, if Danny even knew what an auction was.

"Well," the boy drawled, unconsciously mimicking his father. "I guess that's okay then."

Kate looked up at Dustin. "See ya."

"Yeah." He glanced at her lips and then frowned. "How many hours until tomorrow night?"

"Too many. Bye." Falling in love was ridiculous, she knew, but it was also the best thing that had happened to her in a long time. She watched him leave, watched Danny dump a load of metal vehicles by the back door, and thought she'd never been happier. And that meant, according to her one experience with falling in love, that something was about to go dreadfully wrong.

Or maybe, she thought, going back into the kitchen, she'd been writing soap opera story lines for too long. Maybe she didn't recognize something normal and uncomplicated when it landed in her lap.

GERT SAW THE WOMAN first. She'd dozed off in the chair, but she woke when she heard the car. Even an old woman could hear a car with no muffler when it chugged up the road. So she wasn't too surprised when the woman who got out of the driver's side of the car looked pretty scraggly. Gert didn't think she'd ever seen her before.

"Kate?" Gert didn't like the looks of this. Too many years living alone gave her a suspicious nature, especially when a beat-up station wagon with a tough-looking young woman entered the ranch yard. "*Kate.*"

"What?" She poked her head in the living room. "What's wrong?"

"Someone's here and I don't like the look of her."

"Her?"

Gert pointed to the window. The young woman took a final drag of her cigarette and tossed it to the ground before walking toward the front door.

"You don't know her?"

"No, but that doesn't mean anything. I forget faces once in a while." Gert hauled herself to her feet. "Where's Danny?"

"Out back with his trucks. I gave him a bucket of water and he's dug a hole—"

"You answer the door then," Gert said. "I'm going to check on the boy. Keep the screen door locked, though. Don't open it and let her in. You just never know these days."

Kate was at the door when the knock came, and she opened it and peered through the screen at a woman her age who looked as if she could use a shower. "Hello?"

"Hi." Pale and very thin, the woman wore her dark hair past her shoulders. A blue T-shirt hung to her hips, and her blue jeans were faded and worn. "Does Dusty Jones work here?"

"He's not here right now. Can I give him a message?" The woman looked familiar, but Kate couldn't come up with a name to fit the face.

"But he works here, right? That's what they told me at the Dead Horse." She looked around the yard as if she expected Dustin to come around the corner of the house.

"He works here," Kate agreed. "But he's not here right now." She tried again. "Can I give him a message?"

Once again Kate was ignored. "You're Kate

McIntosh. I know you.'' She smiled, but it wasn't the kind of smile that made Kate relax. ''I'm Lisa Gallagher.'' She chuckled. ''Well, I *was* Lisa Gallagher and then I was Lisa Jones.''

''Sure,'' Kate said slowly, but she didn't open the screen door and invite Lisa inside. ''I remember you from high school.''

''I came for Danny,'' the woman said. ''I had a little trouble, but I got out of rehab and here I am,'' she announced, as if she expected Kate to be happy to see her. ''So tell my kid that his mom is here.''

Kate hesitated. *Rehab?* Danny's words rang in her head. *My mom drank a lot of beer. We don't have a family.* The child rarely mentioned his mother, and Dustin hadn't said anything good about her either. She didn't think he'd want Danny to see her unless he gave his permission.

''I don't think so,'' Kate said, attempting a pleasant smile. ''He's with his father.''

''His father?'' Her confused expression cleared. ''Oh, you mean Dusty.''

''Yes. They went to Marysville.'' Let Lisa head somewhere else to make trouble, because Kate just knew this woman was up to no good.

''I saw Dusty in town. Alone.'' Lisa moved closer to the door and raised her voice. ''So where's my kid?''

''He's not here.'' Kate thought about shutting the inner door in her face, but worried that Lisa would head around back and find her son. She hoped Gert brought the boy inside and locked the back door behind her.

Her eyes narrowed. "You lying bitch. You have my son and I want him. Dusty has no right to keep him from me." She tried to push the door, but Kate had made sure the screen door was locked.

"That's it," Kate said. "Get out of here." She shut the inner door, locked it, and hurried through the house to the back door. Gran had Danny by the hand in the kitchen, so Kate rushed across the room to make sure the door was locked.

"Is my mom here?" Danny's eyes were huge in his little face.

Kate sighed. The woman pounded on the back door and yelled Danny's name. "Yes. I guess she's upset. She wants to see you, but—"

The child nodded and threw himself into Kate's arms. "Don't let her take me away," he cried. "I want to stay here."

"I called the sheriff's office," Gert said. "They're going to send someone over as soon as they can."

Meanwhile the screaming continued at the back door. Lisa was threatening to sue everyone and make sure Dustin never saw Danny again. Kate knelt on the floor and gave Danny a hug. "No one's going to let her take you away from your daddy," she promised.

"She's mean," he whispered. "And she was in jail 'cuz she hurt me. And she took drugs. And my *real* daddy's in jail 'cuz he took drugs, too, and he hid it in our house and then the police came."

"Real daddy?" Kate looked at Gert, who shrugged. "I thought Dustin was your daddy."

The child shook his head. "I *pretend* Uncle Dustin is my daddy," he whispered, then wrapped his arms around Kate's neck in a viselike grip as Lisa's shouting grew louder. "He lets me."

"Well, I told your…daddy that I would take good care of you, so we're all going to go upstairs," Kate told the two of them. She would think about this "Uncle Dustin" revelation later. "There's no reason why we have to listen to this. Danny, you run up there and watch for the sheriff's car, okay? I'll help Grandma Gert."

"Okay." He hugged her and then did as he was told.

"I have my grandfather's hunting rifle," Gert muttered, opening the utility closet. "I can't remember where I locked up the bullets, but I'll bet just the sight of it would scare the living daylights out of that woman." She rummaged through the closet and pulled out a rifle that had seen better days.

"Gran, I don't think—"

"Kate, mind your business," Gert said. "The

young woman outside needs to learn some manners.''

"I'm going to call the sheriff again." She picked up the phone and hit the redial button. "Don't shoot anyone, please?"

"I remember now," Gert said, going to the cupboard above the stove. "I locked the bullets up with the liquor." Kate had never seen her grandmother move so fast.

"Gran, I don't think—oh, hello, this is Kate McIntosh out at the Lazy K. Yes, she called a few minutes ago…yes, she's still here. Lisa Gallagher, I mean, Lisa Jones. She's causing a real scene and we're not sure what to do."

"Speak for yourself," Gert muttered, loading the rifle with stiff fingers.

"Great. Thank you." She hung up and eyed her grandmother, who was now heading toward the back door. "Put the rifle down, Gran. Someone's on the way. Besides, I think Lisa's gone."

Gert peeked out the kitchen window. "I don't see her. Check and see if the car's still out front."

It was. Kate saw Lisa sitting on the steps, her head on her knees and her shoulders shaking. She didn't know why she felt sorry for the woman, but Kate opened the front door and went over to her. She didn't dare look up at the front bedroom window, because she knew she'd see her grandmother's rifle. Kate didn't know whether to laugh or cry.

"Lisa?"

She didn't lift her head. "Go away," she mumbled, or at least that's what Kate thought she said.

"You don't have custody of Danny, do you," Kate said, sitting beside her on the wide step.

"No. I'm a lousy mother."

Candid, too. "So why are you here?"

"I just wanted to tell him I was sorry for everything. I'm going to California," she said, raising her head to look at Kate. "A friend there's gonna give me a job in his bar." She sniffed and wiped her face with the edge of her shirt. "I'm sorry I lost my temper. I do that sometimes and it gets me in trouble."

"My grandmother called the sheriff, Lisa. You scared us."

"I just wanted to see my kid."

"He's afraid of you, especially after all that yelling." Kate thought for a moment. "Would you like to write him a note? I'll see that he gets it."

"That'd probably be better, I guess."

"I'll be right back." Kate went inside and grabbed a legal pad and a pen from Gert's desk, then hurried back outside. She handed them to Lisa and then returned to the house to assure Danny and Gert that everything was okay. Danny was under her bed and didn't want to come out, so Kate left him there while she convinced Gert to unload the rifle.

Three minutes later she went back outside to find Lisa waiting by her car and the notepad and pen on the front steps.

"Thanks," Lisa said, pulling her hair back into a ponytail and securing it with a leather strip. "Tell Danny I won't be back."

"I will."

"Dusty will be really pissed when he finds out I was here. Can you explain it to him?" She opened the car door and slid in behind the wheel.

"Sure. If you explain something to me." Lisa nodded. "You weren't pregnant with Dustin's baby nine summers ago, were you?"

Lisa's eyebrows rose. "Not me. I had the hots for Darrell, his older brother. We got married." She grimaced. "What a mistake that was. When we weren't trying to drink ourselves to death, we were doing coke."

"And what about Danny?"

"When we got arrested, that's when Dusty found out what was going on and took Danny. He's not a bad kid, but when you're a junkie, having a kid around is a real pain in the ass." With that, she turned the key in the ignition and Kate backed away and let her leave.

When Kate looked back at the house, sure enough, Gert still had the rifle in the window. Sheriff Jess Sheridan, arriving five minutes later, turned out to be the only person who could get Gert to put down the gun once and for all.

"WHAT DO YOU WANT to do?"

"I dunno."

Kate lay on her stomach beside Danny underneath the iron bed that used to belong to her mother. The boy stretched out beside her, his chin resting on his folded arms. She wished she knew the magic words that would comfort him. He'd been under the bed for an hour, even after being reassured that his mother had gone away for good. "Want to go for a walk?"

"Nope."

She slid the plate of cookies closer to him. "Help yourself." The boy hesitated, then reached out to take one.

"I'm glad I cleaned under here," Kate said, hoping to make him smile. "Otherwise you'd be eating dust bunnies."

He didn't smile, but at least he still had his appetite. "When's my dad coming home?"

"Tonight. After supper, I would think." She'd thought about having the sheriff find him at the auction, but maybe this way was better, with Danny having a chance to calm down and the three of them going on with their afternoon as they'd planned.

"You still making ice cream?"

"*We're* still making ice cream," she said.

"When?"

"When we get out from under the bed."

Danny sighed and closed his eyes. "Not yet, okay?"

"Okay." Kate was more than willing to wait until the little boy wasn't afraid anymore. And oddly enough, lying on the floor under the bed, a curtain of white chenille fringe surrounding them, made a good place to think.

So Dustin had been lying to her all along. Well, maybe he'd never come right out and said it, but he certainly hadn't explained that he was the child's uncle. He'd let her think he got Lisa pregnant. But why? Because that was an easy way to break up with her so many years ago? An easy way to get rid of the gawky girl who thought he was her first love?

Kate looked over at Danny, who had fallen asleep with a half-eaten cookie in his hand. She wanted to smooth the hair from his face, but was afraid she'd disturb him. He was a sweet boy who needed a mother. Maybe that's what Dustin wanted this time, a mother for the boy and—as a bonus— his own ranch. Not bad for a man who never had much of anything of his own.

She wanted to be angry, but she felt more like crying. *Loves of Our Lives* was simple compared to the goings-on in Beauville. She'd return her boss's phone calls later on. She'd book herself a seat on the first flight to New York Saturday and from now on she'd never look back. Gran would finish her book; Mom could have her mysterious nervous breakdowns, her real estate developer and her new apartment; Jake would have more babies; Emily would have her tubes tied; and life would go on.

Kate didn't think she'd be taking many more vacations in Texas.

CHAPTER TWENTY

DUSTIN ARRIVED BACK at the ranch feeling pretty good about the heifers he'd bought. Gert was going to like the price, too.

"Hello?" he called at the back door, but there was no answer and the door was locked. Good thing the animals weren't going to be delivered until Saturday, or he'd be herding cows all by himself tonight.

There was a note tacked on the bunkhouse, informing Dustin that the women and Danny had taken food over to Jake and Elizabeth's ranch and would be back later, before dark. He would clean up and get some paperwork done before they returned.

He was pleased with the way the afternoon went. Danny was going to get a large pony named Boomer, outgrown by his previous owner. Kate was going to get a marriage proposal. And poor Martha McIntosh was going to get a cowboy for a son-in-law, if Dustin was lucky.

And he felt pretty damn lucky.

"YOU'RE LUCKY SHE didn't hurt you," Gran said, still fuming over Lisa's invasion of the home place. She waved goodbye to Danny, who had paused at the door of the bunkhouse as Dustin held the door open for him to go inside.

"I told you, I felt sorry for her," Kate said, turning the car around. The headlights swept across the windows she knew were part of Dustin's bedroom. She wouldn't be spending any more time in that room.

"Better she should have seen my gun."

"Gran, for heaven's sake. You've got to get rid of that thing. At least get it out of the closet and put it in the attic."

"I keep the bullets locked up," she muttered. "But all right, you can put the rifle away. I guess you'll know where it is when you need it."

It would have been a good time to tell her she wasn't staying, but Kate figured her grandmother could wait another day to be disappointed. She hadn't come up with the right way to tell her yet, either. Hopefully, after a long night thinking about this, she would think of the least painful way to leave.

"Jake's baby is beautiful," Kate said, hoping to change the subject. "She looks just like Elizabeth."

"She does," Gran agreed. "She's a good little

thing. Snuggled in my arms like she belonged there.''

"How does it feel to be a great-grandmother?"

"I'm glad I lived long enough to see it," she said. "Jake will be a good father."

"Yes." Her cousin was as devoted a husband and father as she'd ever seen. Jake had always been the steady one, the man everyone depended on in a crisis. The last man in the family.

"I didn't know Dustin was that little boy's uncle," Gran said, shaking her head. "But I knew something wasn't quite right."

"Why?" She parked the car and opened the door to illuminate the interior, then gathered up the empty casserole dishes.

"He'd never had a chocolate milk shake."

"What?"

"Never mind. It was just something that struck me as odd at the time. And he said those strange things about his family, remember?"

"Yes." And Dustin hadn't explained. Not a word. He'd let her go on thinking he'd made Lisa pregnant, let her go on assuming that he had married and divorced the woman, that he had a son. He hadn't been honest. Again. And she supposed that's what hurt the most. He'd let her into his bed but not into his life.

It was exactly what happened nine years ago.

"Kate?"

"Oh, sorry," she said, and hurried over to help Gran out of the car. "I guess I'm tired."

"I guess we both are," Gran said, "but your cowboy is heading our way, so you'd better perk up. He's going to want to know what happened here today."

"Danny must have told him."

"You're going to give him the letter?"

Kate nodded and helped her grandmother cross the gravel drive and negotiate the path to the kitchen door. "He can decide what to do with it."

"He's not going to like any of this," Gran warned.

"I don't either," Kate said and braced herself.

"Danny told me Lisa was here," Dustin said, following them into the kitchen. "I can't stay long," he added, with a glance toward Kate, "but I wanted to thank both of you for taking care of him this afternoon. I'm really sorry she scared you. She has a mean temper when she gets going."

"We wouldn't let anything happen to that boy. And we were fine, didn't even need the sheriff," Gert said, patting his arm. "I'm off to bed. Come over in the morning and tell me all about our new cattle. I assume you bought some?"

"I sure did," Dustin said, standing close to Kate. She moved away from him. "Good night, Gert."

"Good night, Dustin. That boy of yours did just

fine," she said, before she left the room and headed for her bedroom.

"What a mess," he said, turning to Kate. "I'm really sorry you had to deal with it."

"Lisa wrote a letter to Danny." Kate moved away and reached on top of the refrigerator for the legal pad. "Here. I suggested she write to him instead of trying to talk to him, so I hope you don't mind."

He took the pad and glanced at the brief note. "Fair enough. Danny said she's going away?"

"Yes." She took a deep breath. "We both are."

His eyes narrowed. "You want to explain that?"

"Not necessarily. I don't think you've wanted to explain things to me either. Not about Danny's father and mother. Not about who he really was, or who you really are. So I guess we're even." She managed to keep her voice from trembling.

"Just like that," he said. "You're going back to New York?"

"Yes. I'm flying out first thing Saturday." She looked away, hoping that he wouldn't see how much she was hurt. "Gran will sell you the ranch, I'm sure."

"Yeah." She could hear the anger in his voice. "When you decide to leave, you don't waste a hell of a lot of time, do you?"

She didn't know how to answer, but then again, she didn't think he expected her to say anything.

"I should have learned the first time," he muttered and walked out the door.

"Me, too," Kate said, and this time she let herself cry.

"THIS IS ALL WRONG." Gert rearranged her papers again, then poured herself another cup of coffee to take back to her chair. "I don't like this a bit, young lady." She didn't understand young people. How foolish could they be? Didn't they know how quickly time passed?

"I'm sorry, Gran." Kate finished washing the breakfast dishes and dried her hands. "But I have to leave."

"Nonsense. You and that young man can patch things up." Kate didn't fool her grandmother. The girl wasn't leaving because of her fancy job. Why, she'd only returned a couple of the dozen or so phone calls she'd gotten from New York. And she'd stopped watching the show on TV after the first couple of days.

"I don't think so."

"Where's the boy this morning?"

"George Bennett picked him up. He's taking the boys fishing for the day. I guess John's gotten tired of having a new sister."

"Sounds nice," Gert said. "Means Dustin's free to talk some sense into you." She leaned forward to look out the window. "Oh, dear. Here comes your mother with that Jackson fella. I sure hope she isn't having one of her fits."

"Me, too." Kate stepped into the living room and eyed the piles of paper. "What decade are you in? I'm going into Marysville today to buy you your own laptop and printer so you can take your time finishing the book."

"Aw, hon, that's real nice, but—" She looked out the window again. "They're raisin' a lot of dust, and the sheriff is right behind them. Do you think it's one of them high-speed chases like they have in California?"

Kate hurried over to the window. "Is that *Jake*'s truck?"

"It's a regular parade," Gert declared, hauling herself out of her chair. There was no reason getting upset until there was something to get upset over. "I'd better make a fresh pot of coffee. Looks like we're getting company."

Before she fixed the coffeepot, she hung the red rag in the back window to summon her foreman. She might need some help and Kate might need a man. A woman never knew when one would come in handy.

"REMEMBER HOW I told you there was a dead body in the drive-in?" Martha wrung her hands and looked at everyone gathered around her mother's kitchen table, except for Dustin Jones, who leaned against a wall and looked like he'd rather be anywhere else but inside this house. That nice sheriff thanked Kate for his coffee and acted like he was here on a social call, but Martha knew different. She'd be arrested by noon and all hell would break loose. Her picture would make the front page of the next issue of the *Beauville Times* and it would be all grainy and make her look twenty years older and thirty pounds heavier.

"Mom," Kate said, reaching out to take one of her hands, "are you sure you—"

"I'm sure," Martha said, giving Kate's fingers a little squeeze before she took her hand away. "Carl's offered to dig it—him—up. If I want him to. But he has to do it soon or miss his window of opportunity."

"Dig *who* up, Martha?" her mother asked. Martha couldn't look at her mother. This really wasn't going to be a very good morning.

"Excuse me," that nice Sheriff Sheridan interjected. He gave her a kind smile. "Why don't we make this an unofficial conversation? You could say something like, 'what if?' and we could all assume you were just asking for information and not making an actual confession."

Carl nodded. "That's a good idea, Martha. Start over again."

"Okay." She took a deep breath and looked at the sheriff. "What if I—I mean, *someone*—helped someone else bury a dead person so no one would know he'd been killed?''

Jess Sheridan looked thoughtful. ''I guess that would depend on the circumstances.''

''Mother, what about calling a lawyer?''

Martha shook her head. ''*What if* someone had a best friend—'' She glanced at her nephew, who stared at her as if he'd never seen her before. ''A best friend,'' she repeated, ''whose husband couldn't hold his liquor.'' She heard her mother's quick intake of breath but didn't dare look in her direction. ''And he beat her. A lot. And when he found out she was pregnant he threatened to kill her.''

Kate handed her a tissue, so Martha wiped her eyes. She hadn't wanted to cry, but the whole thing was really getting to be too upsetting.

''Oh, Lord,'' she heard Gert mutter.

''*What if,* uh, this person hit her husband with a frying pan, one of those cast-iron pans?'' Everyone nodded. They knew cast iron. ''Accidentally, of course,'' she added.

''Of course,'' Kate agreed.

''As in self-defense,'' the sheriff said.

''Yes, that's it.'' She blew her nose. ''Then, *what if* that person called her very best friend and asked for help and they didn't know what to do because they were pretty young and one was pregnant and they were both very scared and neither one wanted the baby to be born in jail—'' Here, at this part, she couldn't help looking at Jake, hoping he would understand.

"Go on, Aunt Martha," he told her. "It'll be all right."

"Mrs. McIntosh," Jess said, his voice low and very casual, "let me ask you this. If someone was going to get rid of someone's friend's husband's body, where would someone put it?"

"Maybe in an old well on someone's great-great-grandfather's ranch that became a drive-in."

"And where is the best friend now, the one that was pregnant?"

"She died in 1982."

"And the alcoholic abusive husband who was killed accidentally in self-defense, what year was that?"

Martha opened her mouth to speak, but it was Gert who answered. "I would imagine that was March of '65, Sheriff. And the only one who might have missed him was his mother."

"And his son?" Jake had gone very, very pale.

Martha's heart ached for him, but she didn't know what else to say to make him feel better. "No," Martha said. "His son was better off without him."

Gert eyed the sheriff. "Well, I guess you've heard quite a story today."

"Is this going in your book, Gert?" He stood

and slid his chair into place, then put on his Stetson.

"No. Is it going in yours?"

Martha held her breath when he looked at her.

"Well, let me put it this way. If someone found a body, I'd have to investigate. It probably would be real hard to figure out what happened though, considering how that, uh, incident occurred in 1965." He cleared his throat and turned to Gert. "If someone wanted to leave well enough alone, maybe fill in that well, then that'd be the end of it. All I heard here this morning was some unofficial conversation."

"Thank you," Martha said. If Gert and Jake understood, she would probably be able to sleep tonight—unless Carl insisted on staying over again. "I thought you'd arrest me."

He smiled and headed toward the door, but stopped to pat her on the shoulder. "No, ma'am. Not unless you insist."

"IS THERE ANYTHING else you'd like to tell us, Martha?" Gert certainly hoped there wasn't. She'd always known, deep in her heart, that her only son, Hank, had come to a bad end. And she could admit that it was a relief to find out he hadn't taken anyone else with him. She'd always been afraid he'd died driving drunk, with innocent victims dead on the road because of it.

"Well," Martha said, fidgeting with her hands again.

"Mother?" Kate had gone pale. "You mean there's *more?*"

"Your grandmother started it," Martha protested, "with all this talk of history and town secrets and buried treasure. What was I supposed to do? Wait for Hank to get dug up?"

"Please," Jake said, briefly closing his eyes. "My mother never said much about my father, but—"

"He wasn't your father," Martha said.

Jake frowned. "If he wasn't my father, then who was?"

"You really don't know?"

"Aunt Martha, if I knew I wouldn't be sitting here asking."

"Ah," Gert sighed. "Of course."

Kate looked at her. "Of course what?"

Gert smiled at her grandson, who technically wasn't her grandson at all. "You can't guess?"

Jake shook his head. "Not R.J."

"Yes," Martha said. "He and your mother were very much in love. He would have married her, but she didn't think it was proper for a man as wealthy as R. J. Calhoun to marry his housekeeper. She was old-fashioned that way."

"And he left you his mother's ranch," Gert said. "Now it all makes sense."

Carl cleared his throat. "May I say something?"

Since he hadn't spoken since he'd arrived, Gert figured it was only fair he get a word in now.

"Go ahead," she told him.

"It's about the well, and the, uh, body," he said, with a quick glance at Gert. "What do you all want me to do? I halted construction this morning—told the men I had to get another permit—but I'm gonna have to start up again sooner or later and I have to know what to do about that well."

Gert noticed that Dustin was trying to sidle toward the back door. She wasn't going to let him stand by and let Kate leave without a fight, especially not now. "Dustin?"

"Yes, ma'am?"

"We're all going to the Good Night Drive-In. You and Kate are going to take me in the Lincoln."

Neither one of them protested, which was a darn good thing, too, because Gert had had enough aggravation for one morning.

"GET OUT," KATE SAID. "Now."

Dustin made no move to get out of the car. He rested one wrist on the steering wheel and acted as if he had all the time in the world to sit there and look at her. "That sounds familiar. *Get out.* That's what you told me that night I came to pick you up to go to the movies. *Get out,* you said. Just like that.''

''You could have told me the rumors about you and Lisa weren't true.'' She looked out the side window and prayed that her grandmother would return soon. Jake, Gran and Mom were huddled in the distance, where Kate assumed the well was— where Uncle Hank was. Gert had ordered her and Dustin to stay put and keep anyone from snooping around.

Not that there would be anyone snooping around, not at noon in the summer, in the middle of an empty construction site.

''If I'd had any idea what you were talking about,'' Dustin said, which made Kate turn to look at him again.

''You *had* to know,'' she said.

He shrugged. ''I didn't even live at home that summer. I worked out at the Dead Horse six days a week, from dawn 'til dinnertime. I only came into town to see you.'' He paused. ''You never even asked me if it was true, Kate. You just believed that I'd gotten someone pregnant instead of believing that I loved you too much to do something like that.''

''You never said you loved me. You said 'no strings,' and 'we'll just have fun.'''

''I lied.''

She held his gaze with her own. "You seem to be good at it."

"I was going to tell you about Danny," he said, having the decency to look guilty. "I guess at first I thought you didn't deserve the truth. And later on there never seemed to be the right time to go into the whole story." He smiled. "Making love got in the way."

She wished he hadn't reminded her of that. "I loved you, too, a long time ago."

"And now?" He reached over and took her hand.

"No."

"Now who's lying?"

Kate shook her head. "It's not going to work, Dustin. You know it's not."

"You're running away again, Katie," he said, planting a kiss in her palm. "You ran away from me. Why?"

"I loved you. You didn't love me. Simple."

"And you ran away from town after your dad died."

She turned away and wished he would release her hand. She should go check on her mother and her grandmother. And she bet Jake could use a hug right now. What on earth could they be talking about for such a long time?

"Kate?"

"What?"

"Stay and love me." He tugged her across the wide seat of the Lincoln and against that hard wide chest. "I've been waiting for you to come back for nine years."

"Liar," she whispered, but she smiled against his chest.

"It's true." Dustin lifted her away from him and looked down into her eyes. "I want to marry you, even though your grandmother thinks she's going to be famous and your mother helped bury a dead body and my son likes you more than he does me—"

"That's not true. He worships the ground you walk on."

"Yeah?"

She nodded. "He told me that his other daddy hit him all the time, but you just make a frowny face."

"And that's a good thing?"

"Definitely. And my grandmother is actually writing a very good book."

"I'll believe it when I see it," he said, and with one easy motion lifted her over the seat and into the back. He climbed over the leather upholstery to join her as she scrambled to sit up.

"What are you doing? There are people around. They'll be back any—"

He kissed her then, his hands holding her face to his, until she melted against him. Habit, she thought. Making love in cars was a very dangerous habit.

"Marry me," he said, lifting his mouth a fraction of an inch. "We'll conceive our first child in the back seat of any vehicle you choose."

"Second child," she reminded him. "Danny's the first."

"That's a 'yes?'"

"Uh-huh," she said, wrapping her arms around his neck. "You get me, the ranch, my mother and my grandmother. What do I get?"

The damn cowboy grinned. "Take your jeans off and I'll show you."

Kate looked out the window. "Too late. Here they come. Hurry up, get back in the front seat."

He grabbed her wrist as she started to straddle the front seat. "Are you going to marry me or not?"

"Kate!" Martha's voice carried across the wind. "What on earth are you doing?"

"Discussing my honeymoon," she shouted, and saw her mother's mouth fall open. Gran waved and Jake gave her a "thumb's up" sign.

Gran came over to the car. "You two stay there and work things out. Martha and I will get a ride home with Jake." She winked. "Take your time. I've got a lot of writing to do this afternoon and Martha's going to help me with the 1980s."

"Okay." Kate tumbled into the back seat again.

"Now," she said, moving toward her new fiancé, "you were going to show me something?"

He chuckled, his mouth against hers, as they tumbled backward. Kate landed on top of him, which was a very satisfactory place to be.

"Do you think it's right to leave them here like this?" Kate heard her mother complain. Jake chuckled.

"Martha," Gert snapped, "leave the children alone. We need a couple of cold beers and a box of tissues and a good long talk, so keep walking and mind your own business."

Dustin tilted his head to whisper in Kate's ear, "Isn't that the pot calling the kettle black?"

Kate laughed when she kissed him. It was so good to be home.

EPILOGUE

"TELL YOUR MOM I have big news," Martha announced, pleased that little Danny had answered the phone so promptly. That boy was growing up. She'd bet he'd shot up two inches this past year and a half since his father married Kate.

"Really, Grammy? *What* big news?"

"Grown-up stuff, Danny. Where's your mother?" Martha liked it that he called her "Grammy." She thought she'd mind at first, but she'd discovered she really liked the sound of that word. And with Kate seven-and-a-half months' pregnant, it was a good thing she'd gotten used to being a grandmother so quickly.

"Here," the boy said, and Martha heard the rustling of papers and her daughter's voice in the background.

"Mother? Hi. What's going on? I thought we were going to meet later on in—"

"We still are," Martha assured her. "If you're feeling up to it."

"I wouldn't miss it, you know that. What's this big news?"

"Jake and Elizabeth are expecting again," she announced. "Isn't that wonderful? Your babies will grow up together." Martha chatted a little bit more, pleased to have been the first one to tell Kate the news, but she didn't stay on the phone long. She'd been satisfied to hear her daughter's voice and know that she and the baby were doing all right.

You couldn't be too careful these days, Martha thought, looking out the window of her corner apartment. It was a nice place. Carl had seen to it that she had one of the larger units with a view of the back acreage. He'd sulked a little bit when she'd refused to marry him—he'd sure wanted to move in to the house on Apple Street—but he'd accepted her decision to sell the house to Emily. She and George and their growing family could use the space.

Martha had grown tired of cleaning all those rooms. Her spacious one-bedroom villa, with its panoramic views and ivory wall-to-wall carpet suited her just fine. Living alone suited her just fine, too, but sometimes she let Carl spend the night. Just for fun.

She glanced at her watch. Mother would be waiting for her. And Mother didn't like to be kept waiting these days.

"HOW MANY DAYS?" Danny asked, watching Kate take another batch of sugar cookies out of the oven.

"Until Christmas? Nineteen," she replied, accustomed to the question Danny asked daily. "In nineteen days we'll open presents Christmas morning, with Grandma Gert and Grammy, right here in our house."

"Our house," he whispered, smiling up at her with such joy that Kate immediately choked up. She felt that way often these days, as the baby grew bigger and the boy more affectionate and her husband more protective. She managed to slide each cookie off the tray and onto a cooling rack before Dustin came downstairs and entered the kitchen.

"Are we ready?" He tousled Danny's hair and gave Kate a hug. "Mmm," he said. "You smell like vanilla."

"Mom's makin' sugar cookies," Danny said, "for the party at school. We're gonna decorate them tomorrow."

Dustin's arms tightened around her and he rested his chin on the top of her head. "You okay?"

"Never better," she managed to say, though her husband looked down and his gaze softened at the tears she was trying so hard to hide. "We're going to be late."

"Gert will wait for us," Dustin said.

"I'm not so sure. She's a big star now." Kate shifted sideways so she could snuggle closer to her husband. She couldn't imagine living anywhere but on the ranch. She never missed her life in New York; instead, she submitted story concepts, via e-mail, to her boss. Two had been accepted this fall, meaning she and Dustin would be able to start on the new horse barn, and Danny's college account had begun. But she was happy letting Gran take the stage as the writer in the family. "Gran loves the attention."

"As long as she doesn't get too big for Beauville," he said.

"Please don't say the words 'too big' around a very pregnant woman," Kate told him, and hugged her husband even tighter. "Or I'll never get in the back seat of a car with you again."

THE MEMBERS OF THE newly formed Beauville Book Club gathered together for the December meeting in the Good Night Villas' library. It was actually the southwest meeting room, but the members of the book club liked to refer to it as the library on the days they met.

Gert fiddled with her notes.

So far she'd taken all this hoopla in stride, selling her book to a Texas publishing house, moving to the Villas and even signing a television deal with The History Channel.

But speaking in front of all these gabbing women, women who couldn't sit still for more than fifteen minutes without having an opinion, was something else all together. So Gert gripped her notes and walked over to the window that over-looked the west end of the Villas' property.

After the well had been filled in, she and Martha had covered the top with some pretty flowers. Gert liked being close to Hank this way. At least she knew he was safe and she felt better knowing where he was buried.

Gert liked looking after him.

Irene Bennett called the meeting to order as Kate, Dustin and Danny slipped into seats in the back. Jake and Elizabeth, bless them, were in the second row. They must have gotten a sitter for lit-tle Nancy, which was a good idea. Gert didn't know if she could talk loud enough to compete with that happy little girl of theirs.

Martha waved to her, gesturing that it was time for her mother to go to the podium. She'd finished stacking the copies of *A Woman Remembers* on a nearby folding table. Irene was pretty long-winded, though, so Gert didn't rush. No one could make a ninety-one-year-old woman hurry across a room, no matter how loud the applause.

"Thank you," she told her audience. "I'm real pleased to have my books here. And I'm real pleased to see my family." She took a deep breath and read from the notes she'd tucked inside a copy of her book.

"From the Comanche raids of 1850, to the Civil War and later, when the railroad came, my family was here. Here fighting to survive and prosper, to raise their children and build a town. Somehow they managed to survive, despite all the hardships thrown their way." Gert paused and looked for the faces of her own family. *My, my, this might be fun after all,* she thought. She opened her book and turned to page one. Holding one gnarled finger on the page, she cleared her throat and then began to read, "I blame it all on Texas…"

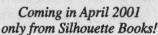

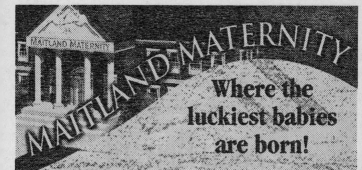

MAITLAND MATERNITY

Where the luckiest babies are born!

In April 2001, look for

HER BEST FRIEND'S BABY

by Vicki Lewis Thompson

A car accident leaves surrogate mother Mary-Jane Potter's baby-to-be without a mother—

and causes the father, Morgan Tate, to fuss over a very pregnant Mary-Jane like a mother hen. Suddenly, Mary-Jane is dreaming of keeping the baby...and the father!

Each book tells a different story about the world-renowned Maitland Maternity Clinic— where romances are born, secrets are revealed... and bundles of joy are delivered.

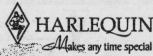

From bestselling
Harlequin American Romance author

CATHY GILLEN THACKER

comes

TEXAS VOWS

A McCABE FAMILY SAGA

Sam McCabe had vowed to always
do right by his five boys—but after
the loss of his wife, he needed the small-town security
of his hometown, Laramie, Texas, to live up to that
commitment. Except, coming home would bring him
back to a woman he'd sworn to stay away from.
It will be one vow that Sam can't keep....

On sale March 2001

Available at your favorite retail outlet.

HARLEQUIN®
Makes any time special ™

Visit us at www.eHarlequin.com

PHTV

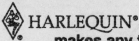

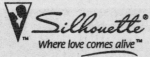